ORNITHOLOGY

BY THE SAME AUTHOR

NOVELS

Counterparts
Saxophone Dreams
The Matter of the Heart
The Director's Cut
Antwerp
Regicide
First Novel

NOVELLAS

The Appetite
The Enigma of Departure

SHORT STORIES

Mortality
In Camera (with David Gledhill)

ANTHOLOGIES (as editor)

Darklands
Darklands 2
A Book of Two Halves
The Tiger Garden: A Book of Writers' Dreams
The Time Out Book of New York Short Stories
The Ex Files: New Stories About Old Flames
The Agony & the Ecstasy: New Writing for the World Cup
Neonlit: Time Out Book of New Writing
The Time Out Book of Paris Short Stories
Neonlit: Time Out Book of New Writing Volume 2
The Time Out Book of London Short Stories Volume 2
Dreams Never End
'68: New Stories From Children of the Revolution
Best British Short Stories 2011
Murmurations: An Anthology of Uncanny Stories About Birds
Best British Short Stories 2012
Best British Short Stories 2013
Best British Short Stories 2014
Best British Short Stories 2015
Best British Short Stories 2016
Best British Short Stories 2017

ORNITHOLOGY

SIXTEEN SHORT STORIES

NICHOLAS ROYLE

The right of Nicholas Royle to be identified as author of this work has been asserted by him in accordance with the Copyright, Designs and Patent Act 1988.

Copyright © 2017 by Nicholas Royle

All characters in this publication are fictitious and any resemblance to real persons, living or dead, is entirely coincidental.

First published in 2017 by Cōnfingō Publishing
2 Stonecroft, Parkfield Road South, Manchester M20 6DA
Art Direction & Typesetting by Zoë McLean

A CIP catalogue record for this book is available from the British Library
ISBN 978-0-9955966-0-3
Printed by TJ International Ltd.
2 4 6 8 10 9 7 5 3 1

www.confingopublishing.uk

For David Rose

RED KITE

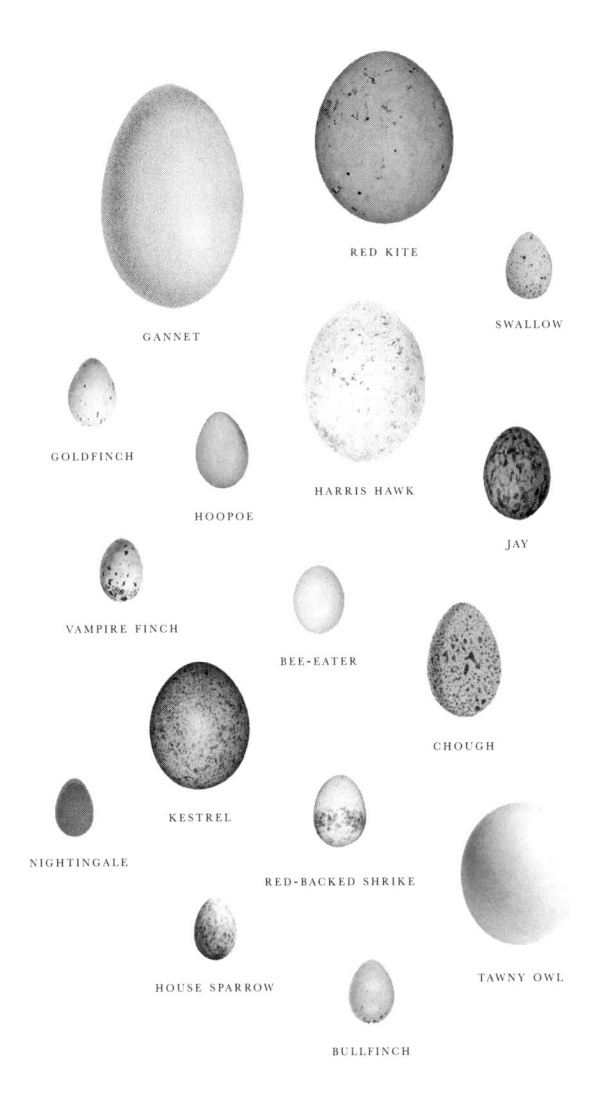

SWALLOW

GANNET

GOLDFINCH

HOOPOE

HARRIS HAWK

JAY

VAMPIRE FINCH

BEE-EATER

CHOUGH

KESTREL

NIGHTINGALE

RED-BACKED SHRIKE

TAWNY OWL

HOUSE SPARROW

BULLFINCH

CONTENTS

UNFOLLOW	11
MURDER	19
THE OBSCURE BIRD	31
JIZZ	41
STUFFED	55
PINK	61
THE BEE-EATER	69
GANNETS	75
THE LARDER	83
THE GOLDFINCH	91
THE KESTREL AND THE HAWK	103
THE LURE	109
THE NIGHTINGALE	135
THE BLUE NOTEBOOKS	151
LOVEBITES	161
THE CHILDREN	171
ACKNOWLEDGEMENTS	189

· UNFOLLOW ·

Max drops his little parcel at my feet, proudly, showing off.

I look. I bend down, not sure what I'm looking at. Out of context, it doesn't make sense. Out of context, nothing makes sense.

It's a bird. Max backs off, job done; he trots into the kitchen.

I look at the bird. It's a sparrow, a juvenile. They say numbers are declining rapidly. The sparrow has been redlisted. No wonder.

I pick it up, turn it over, extend the wings. There's some damage behind the left wing, feathers missing.

In the kitchen I take a small freezer bag from the drawer, drop the bird inside and zip it shut. I place it on the top shelf of the fridge, then climb the stairs to my study and log on to Twitter.

Cat just brought in a sparrow, juvenile. Some damage behind wing. If interested let me know.

I send it as a direct message – to her – then sit staring at the screen as if expecting an instant reply. I find a recent tweet and click on her name to bring up a bigger version of her avatar. Leaning up towards the camera. Raven-black hair tied back, a few strands escaping, curling in front of her ears. Expression ambiguous, halfway between a smile and a sneer. Eyes unreadable, kohl smudges.

I get up and look out of the window. A neighbour walks

past. One of many. I recognise her, but I don't, if you see what I mean. I don't know her name, I'm not even sure where she lives. One of the houses down the road. She's a neighbour. That's all.

I am about to move away from the window when I see another woman walking up the road in the same direction. Another neighbour. She's about thirty yards behind the first one. I wonder if she's following her.

I sit back down at my desk and look at the screen. She has not replied. The Friends column is full of the usual meaningless noise and shameless plugs from people I would unfollow if only I could be bothered. Some stranger replies to a random tweet and you follow them on the off-chance they might have something interesting to say. Something worthwhile to offer. A surreal observation, a satirical remark, a joke. The first time Max brought in a bird, I tweeted about it, because I didn't know what else to do, who else to tell. It was a greenfinch, a beautiful little bird. Or it had been. Max had rendered it almost unidentifiable by the time he dropped it at my feet and I picked it up, thinking it was one of his toys.

I tweeted and the only reply came from someone calling herself Taxigirl. She asked me to send her the greenfinch if it was in a reasonable state. I tweeted back that it wasn't and asked why she wanted it. She switched to direct messaging and explained that she was a taxidermist and always on the lookout for dead birds and larger animals. She lived in London, she said, where she was more than adequately supplied with pigeons and rats; anything more exotic was hard to come by. Obviously that was a few tweets' worth.

I found her website, which was full of pictures of her

work, but no photographs of her. All I had was her avatar, which she never changed, but I saved it to my desktop and blew it up as far as it would go before pixellating. Her real name was Skye MacMahon.

The next bird Max brought in *was* unidentifiable. I didn't waste Skye's time tweeting about it. If I offered her another mangled corpse, she'd think I didn't understand her, didn't grasp what she wanted. I threw the bird in the bin.

For some time – during the winter months – there were no birds. Max brought nothing in. I found a dead pigeon in the street one day, but it had been half-eaten by foxes, and anyway, Skye had said, she was sorted for pigeons.

I made a hard copy of her avatar using a colour printer and carried it around in my wallet. I imagined her at work on an animal, inserting her slender fingers between the skin and flesh of whatever creature she was stuffing. I could almost hear the moist rustle of the separating tissues and consequent seepage of fluids.

I upgraded my mobile so that I could check Twitter while I was out and have a decent-sized screen for looking at pictures. One in particular.

And then Max brought in the sparrow, juvenile.

Skye Direct Messages me later.

A little damage not massive problem. But I don't work with juveniles. Thanks for thinking of me.

Thanks for thinking of me. How to tell her I've done little else for months?

I stand at the window for a moment. Through the foliage that has started to appear on the trees, I watch more neighbours following each other down the street.

I sit with Max and stroke him and talk to him in a low voice about what I want him to do for me.

Two days later I am woken in the morning by Max's plaintive cry. I go downstairs to find him in the hall. I sit on the bottom step. Between us on the bare floorboards is an adult male goldfinch. I smile at Max and he cocks his head on one side before trotting off into the kitchen to lap at the mixer tap. (He has never drunk water from a bowl. By licking repeatedly at the tap he can make a few drops of water appear, which soon become a trickle. But for Max, I would never have imagined that this would be possible.)

I slip the goldfinch, which is in good condition, with its bee-striped wings and little red face, into a freezer bag. I place it in the fridge between the eggs and the cheese, then run up the stairs, two at a time.

I DM Skye.

Adult male goldfinch with very little damage. Absolutely beautiful. I think you're going to want this. I think this is the one. Let me know.

One hundred and forty characters, dead on.

Later the same day she DMs me a PO Box number in London, adding that she assumes I've had it in the freezer since finding it.

I take it out of the fridge and allow it to slide out of the cool freezer bag into my palm. It feels lighter than air. It's stiff, but the cold hand of death has more to do with that than refrigeration. I'm hoping that with the kill being so fresh, the fridge will have served it as well as the freezer might have done. I stroke the minutely detailed feathers with my fingertips and bring the tiny red face up to my own. I place my lips upon its cheek, knowing that by this time tomorrow the bird will be limp in her hands, rigor mortis worn off. I imagine she'll use a scalpel to draw the faintest of lines from some hidden spot under the wing to its secret conclusion and then she will turn the bird inside out like a glove. In truth I know nothing of how she will work, but I picture her hands moving swiftly and skilfully over the tiny carcass, performing ritual movements.

I read and reread the PO Box address, hoping that it will reveal some clue as to her whereabouts. I address the padded envelope and post it.

She sends me a message not the next day or the day after, but the day after that.

Thanks for the goldfinch. I've frozen it for now. I'm working with an artist, we're looking for bigger birds & animals. Bigger the better. x

I stare at that 'x', that kiss, for what seems like hours, my eye constantly drawn back to it. I feel an urgent fluttering inside my chest or my stomach. Somewhere inside me. I know that taxidermists work only with the outside, the skin, the epidermis. Everything within – the skeleton, flesh, muscles and vital organs – is discarded.

I am in the bathroom when Max brings in the blackbird, a fully grown female. He drops it from his jaws to the tiled floor and paws at it experimentally. The blackbird lies still, but there's a tension in the room. Max and I both wait, each staring at the brown bird on the floor between us. Suddenly it twitches and launches itself, flying straight at the window. Max bolts, then stops in the doorway and looks back, caught in a pose as rigid as something stuffed, hair standing on end. The bird batters the glass with its beak as if trying to break through. I approach and seize it from behind in two hands. My heart is hammering. A quick twist of the neck and it would be mine. Hers. But I hesitate. I tell myself that it's because I don't want to cross a line, but I wonder if it's because it's a female. I imagine a female blackbird to be less attractive to a taxidermist – to this taxidermist – than a male.

I open the window and relax my grip on the bird. It flies towards the trees, unaffected by the loss of feathers, which has left the bathroom resembling the site of a pillow fight.

Max follows up the blackbird with a pigeon, which I know will be of no interest to Skye MacMahon, but his kills are getting bigger. Dumping the bird in the wheelie bin, I watch one of my neighbours walk past the house, followed by another and then another. I go back inside and stand at the bedroom window. I watch the street for the rest of the morning, convinced there's a pattern, something organic.

If I was mildly surprised by the pigeon, I am quite taken aback by the rabbit, which is almost as big as a cat. I don't know if it's wild or a neighbour's pet.

I tickle Max under the chin and the rabbit goes into the freezer in a large plastic carrier bag. Skye MacMahon doesn't reply to my message. I wonder if she's suspicious and either doesn't believe me or thinks I'm hunting down prey myself, for whatever ends I might have. I spend the day standing in front of my windows, front and back, watching. Just watching.

The fox is lying in the middle of the kitchen floor, oddly peaceful. Max sits up straight next to it, his face unreadable. I empty the freezer of any remaining food. There's now a precarious tower of hard, slippery packages on the work surface. Plastic packs of prawns, sausages, chicken thighs. Old takeaway containers filled with leftover homemade soup. I'm going to need a chest freezer.

My neighbours follow each other down the street.

Still she doesn't reply to my messages. I search for Taxi-girl on Twitter, but she has not been tweeting.

Early one morning, a week later, I stand in front of the bathroom mirror, toothbrush in hand. I stop brushing and turn the tap off. I stare beyond my reflection as I listen – intently. The house is silent, but the silence has a peculiar quality, almost electric. Something not quite right.

I slot my toothbrush into its holder and leave the bathroom. I get dressed quickly and quietly before heading downstairs, slowly, taking care not to make any noise.

I hesitate at the foot of the stairs. Left to the kitchen or straight on into the back room? I walk straight ahead.

In the back room, in the middle of the floor, is the prone body of one of my neighbours.

Max sits alongside, his head bobbing up and down as he licks his silky coat.

I wonder how I'm going to do this.

· MURDER ·

With the ocean in front of you and waves crashing only a few feet below, close enough for you to taste the salty spray on the air, Canglass Point feels like one of the ends of the Earth. Great black-backed gulls hang steady in the buffeting wind, the bold curly bracket of their wingspan tipping this way and that, while further out gannets cut through the white space like dashes, before one turns into a W as it dives, then a Y and finally, as it drops into the sea, an almost perfect I.

If you were to climb the rock ledges behind you, they would eventually yield to a plateau of close-cropped grassland 120 feet above the waves that in turn leads to a gentle climb to the top of Slievagh more than 600 feet high. If you're likely to spot the blood-dipped beak of the glossy black chough anywhere on the mainland, you're likely to spot it here, somewhere between hilltop and cliff.

In the middle of the plateau is a hole 150 feet by 100. The only way to approach the edge – on your belly. A sheer drop, the odd grassy ledge from which there's no route back up and only one way down. Narrow bands of black rock forced by unimaginable pressures into a series of looping curves. A jagged archway at the western end leading to the ocean, the deep water clear enough to reveal rocks at the bottom.

If you walked over the edge one night, no one would

ever know. If you ran down the hill on a foggy day, they would never find you. The waves would drag you out into the ocean to become food for fish. Picked clean, your skeleton would disintegrate and sink to the sea bed to be found, maybe, a few pieces anyway, a bone at a time in trawl nets over decades to come.

My friends Alice and John stay in a farmhouse in the west of Ireland every year with their friends Virginia and Donald. The four of them are academics with elevated positions in English departments at various universities – in the north of England in Alice and John's case, while Virginia and Donald live and work in the US.

Academia is meant to be an incestuous world, but if you avoid conferences and turn down ridiculously low-paid offers to work as an external examiner, it can be fairly isolating. I have heard of Humanities departments where nobody knew that a colleague had left, and another where a senior lecturer was challenged on entry to the building since it was believed she had retired. My wife, Diana, is Professor of English and head of department – twin roles that exact a steep price in terms of simple happiness. Nothing pleases me more than hearing her unselfconsciously girlish laughter, whether prompted by TV comedy or dinner party or (still occasionally) something I have said. But laughter is rare; I'm more likely to hear 'I could kill that woman' or 'I despair, I just despair'. My professional life, as a fractional lecturer in creative writing, is less stressful.

I first met Alice at a conference on motivation in crime fiction held at the University of Verona, which marked one of my few forays from southern England, since when we have enjoyed a regular and stimulating correspondence. At first we would write to each other about books and birds, two shared passions. We maintained a week-long exchange of emails in which we talked about collective nouns for different types of birds. We would also discuss Virginia and Donald. I would lightly tease Alice about what I perceived as her tendency always to defer to them. I knew, for instance, that it was always Virginia and Donald who made the farmhouse booking, after which they would invite Alice and John to join them. Virginia and Donald would accept payment of half the rent, but they would handle all dealings with the owners, and gave the impression – or allowed Alice and John to form the understanding – that they were somehow vaguely in control.

Last year, in the early spring, Alice emailed me to ask if Diana and I wished to join them for a week's holiday in the west of Ireland.

'In the farmhouse? Is there room for six?'

Alice explained that she and John, having heard nothing from Virginia and Donald, had taken the initiative and emailed them to say they were thinking of going to the farmhouse again and wanted to check to see what Virginia and Donald's plans were before asking anyone else to join them instead.

'We got a non-commital answer,' Alice wrote. 'I inferred that they didn't really want to go this year, but didn't want to give offence by saying so straight out.'

After which, Alice had let a few weeks go by before asking Diana and me if we wanted to join them.

'You'd love it,' she wrote to me. 'Oystercatchers, rock pipits, even reed buntings. And there's always a murder of crows in the field behind the farmhouse.'

'How many crows make a murder?' I asked.

We decided on three; two would be pushing it.

I said I would talk to Diana and we would look at our diaries.

A week later, Alice telephoned. Virginia and Donald had been in touch to propose the same arrangement as usual.

'Oh,' I said.

'Oh no, you were going to say you would join us, weren't you?'

'Well, I know I hadn't got back to you, but you know how it is,' I said.

'Oh damn! I would much rather we could go with you and Diana.'

'We'll go another year,' I said. 'Don't worry about it.'

I didn't hear from Alice for a while and assumed she was busy, which I certainly was, having agreed to be an external for a neighbouring institution. Plus I was trying to complete a couple of papers for academic journals to bolster my department's RAE submission.

These two papers finally off my desk and with days of unending rain denting any hopes of a decent summer, I emailed Alice to ask how the week in Ireland had gone. She replied with a brief report on bird species spotted. The reed buntings had materialised, also gannets, great black-backed gulls and lots and lots of crows.

'A murder?' I asked.

'Oh yes.'

It continued to rain and although Diana and I ticked the days of August off the calendar, we never really felt that summer had arrived before the leaves started to change colour and the return to university unequivocally announced the arrival of autumn. The new term and the next were busier than ever and when Alice emailed in the spring to ask if we would like to join them for a week in the farmhouse, I didn't even have time to enter into banter about their needing to check first with Virginia and Donald.

The farmhouse is situated on a peninsula. You have to drive through the town – a single street lined with shops and pubs with hand-painted wooden signs – then turn left on to the stone bridge. Once over the river, you head left again. There are fewer houses and the hedgerows are alight with a fiery combination of purple and red fuchsias and bright orange Crocosmia lucifer.

As you approach the end of the peninsula, the road turns a sharp left in front of a shallow bay and after a hundred yards you have to stop to open a gate. Now on private land, you may take pleasure in leaving your safety belt unfastened. The way is rutted; grass grows in a line down the middle of the path. Cows amble in the fields alongside. Like clockwork soldiers, jackdaws march.

In the farmyard, hens will scatter. A marmalade cat may be lying on a bale of silage enjoying the low sunlight. Gravel will crunch beneath your tyres and your handbrake will sound a little like the ratcheting cry of a magpie in the otherwise still air of the late afternoon.

They appeared on the doorstep, Alice implausibly attractive for an academic with her long golden hair, hazel eyes and plump red lips, while John's wide-eyed grin hovered somewhere between boyish enthusiasm and the honest astonishment of a man who still can't quite believe his luck.

We got out of the car, joints creaking after the long drive from Dun Laoghaire. I stretched theatrically, but necessarily; Diana approached the open arms of Alice and fell into her embrace. I shook hands with John, who was as hearty as ever.

A third person had appeared between Alice and John. Blonde, sun-blushed from working outdoors, she was introduced by Alice as Marie, the owner.

'Ah, it's grand to meet you, so,' Marie said, surprising and unsettling us with sudden warmth and hugs.

We all moved back inside where Alice resumed food preparation. She was in the middle of peeling vegetables. John put the kettle on for a cup of tea. Personally I would have killed for a glass of Guinness, but four mugs had been lined up on the work surface. Granted they looked as if they were china, but still.

As he removed the spent tea bags from the pot, John turned to Marie.

'So you put these on the flowerbeds?' he said to her.

'Around the hydrangeas, yes. They work a treat.'

I helped Alice, gathering the potato peelings.

'What about these, Marie?' I asked. 'You must have a compost heap somewhere?'

'Just put them in the back field. The cat'll like them.'

I looked at her and she beamed at me. I turned to Diana, frowning, then looked back at Marie.

'Really?' I said.

'Oh yes, the cat'll like them.'

Neither Diana nor I had ever owned a cat, but I was pretty sure cats didn't eat potato peelings.

Marie eventually left and we opened a bottle of wine. The food was good, the company excellent. Night fell softly around the farmhouse almost without our noticing.

꧁

I awoke to the cawing of crows in the back field. Diana was sleeping quietly. I eased my body out of the unfamiliar bed, grabbed my jeans and a T-shirt and walked softly out of the room.

As I brushed my teeth, I wondered if Alice and John, who now had the much better bedroom upstairs, had previously been obliged to use the one in which Diana and I had slept. It was a strangely inhospitable room, chilly despite the season. The tiled floor was cold underfoot. The convex mattress precluded a decent night's sleep.

Finding the kitchen empty, I wandered outside. The potato peelings still lay in a little pile in the back field where I had thrown them the night before. Obviously the cat was not hungry.

Three or four crows picked at the topsoil in the middle of the field, among them a solitary rook. At this distance, I couldn't see the rook's white snout and identified it by its shaggy silhouette and awkward-looking gait in relation to its sleeker cousins. The birds were behaving against type since it is the rook that is sociable, while the territoriality of crows normally keeps their numbers down.

In the distance, the summit of Knocknadobar was still wreathed in low grey cloud. I imagined huge ravens tumbling acrobatically out of sight, their playful nature belied by their grim demeanour.

Alice was making tea. There was no sign of either Diana or John.

'I love this house,' she said, running her hand along the grain of the worktop.

'I know,' I said.

'No, I *really* love it,' she said, looking out of the window.

I asked about the bedrooms and she confirmed they had

used our room on all previous visits apart from the last one, when Virginia and Donald had sought to make amends for the confusion by offering Alice and John the upstairs suite.

Diana appeared, dressed in loose flowing clothes and wearing a little make-up that helped to make her eyes shine. Her thick reddish-brown hair had gone wavy, as it always seemed to do when we went away anywhere; she hated it, but I loved it. I got up to give her a kiss and felt her body relax against mine. She needed this holiday. Over her shoulder I watched the crows moving about in a random pattern in the back field.

We went to a harbour on the north side of the peninsula where John and Alice swam and Diana read a book (as a reaction against creative writing students' ever-lengthening portfolios she had brought a number of very short novels and was currently rereading Marquez's *Chronicle of a Death Foretold*) while I fished from the rocks, casting out a silver lure and retrieving it, a repeated action that seemed as if it might never end unless I actually caught a fish. This finally happened as Alice and John joined us on the rocks, Alice towelling the ends of her damp hair.

At first I assumed the lure had merely become snagged in weed, which had happened once every five or six casts. But on this occasion the weed pulled back. The rod tip bent and I felt that unique and familiar conflict – the desire to let the fish have its head and take line from the spool, thus extending the fight, balanced against the need to land the fish before it swam into weed.

I managed a few turns on the reel and glimpsed the glimmer of a golden flank turning in the deep water just beyond the rocks. It was a decent size, but beaten. I used the lowest ledge of the rocks to land it and knelt to unhook the lure.

I turned to display my catch to the others, who applauded.

'What is it?' Diana asked.

'It's our dinner,' I said. 'A pollack. Couple more like this and we'll eat well.'

'Really?' Diana's eyes were wide. Perhaps she had thought I might put the fish back.

Alice stepped forward.

'May I?' she said and took the fish from me. She grasped its tail in her right hand and turned it over. In one swift movement, she cracked the top of its head against the nearest rock. I heard Diana gasp and John spoke his wife's name as if in reproach. Alice shrugged and dropped the dead pollack on the rocks. 'Catch some more,' she said, making it sound like a challenge.

Grilled and served with lemon and steamed green beans, pollack proves a more than adequate substitute for cod or haddock. A New Zealand Sauvignon Blanc or a Pinot Grigio will be the perfect accompaniment. At some point as the sky darkens, the house martins and swallows swooping over the back field will be replaced by bats, but you will be unable to identify the moment when this happens, or even if it actually has. The one thing you can be sure of is that the black dots in the background, the murder of crows, will not go away. They may change their configuration, flapping in and out of vision, altering their numbers, but two or three will always remain.

Scented candles will burn, keeping midges and mosquitoes at bay and causing shadows to flicker over faces. Intellectual arguments will ripple back and forth as the precise meanings of words will be debated, assumptions about the nature of existence questioned. Doubts, fears, uncertainties at the back of your mind will fade and retreat, but not quite disappear.

Conversation will turn, as usual, to books, to art, to films. Someone will talk about a black-and-white Czech film they have recently seen made in 1968 but set in the 1930s. They will say it deserves to be better known. Someone else will confess to not liking subtitles. Another person will say that *The Third Man* is their favourite film of all time and you will remember the scene in the Ferris wheel, Harry Lime talking to Holly Martins, describing the people below as dots and asking him if he would really feel any pity if one of them stopped moving for ever.

The four of us in one car, we drove past the harbour where I had caught the pollack and on uphill towards the forest. We passed a rustle of reed buntings dispersing from their perch on a barbed-wire fence. Cows chewed on the long grass, their huge jaws grinding and crushing and it suddenly hit me. Cows. Cattle. *The cattle like them.*

'What are you smiling at?' Diana asked.

I grinned at her. 'I'll tell you later.'

When the road petered out in a pine wood, we left the car and threaded our way between the trees, startling a jay, which clattered away with its telltale white flash.

Diana's question seemed to come out of nowhere.

'Don't you miss being here with your other friends?' she said. 'Only, because you normally come with them.'

I noticed John look at Alice, who merely grunted and made a dismissive gesture with her hand.

Leaving the wood, we tramped through bracken to the unmarked summit of Slievagh. Soon after we began our descent on the seaward side, I noticed a strange black disc on the surface of the promontory ahead of us. It reminded me of the black rubber mat a bowls player will drop on the green before starting to play. Because of the changing angle of slope and the lack of other topographical features, it was difficult to tell the size. I was walking with Diana; Alice and John had pulled ahead. We exchanged shrugs, puzzled looks.

It soon became obvious it was a hole, but how deep? Was it merely the result of peat cutting? Or a landslip? It was too big for a pothole. Once we reached the plateau, the narrow angle meant the hole resembled a sheet of water sitting on the grass. Alice and John had reached the edge and were looking down. It took Diana and me a minute or so to join them and finally get a look over the edge.

'It's a long way down,' Diana said.

Alice and John smiled.

'There's an easier way down to the sea over there,' John joked, pointing to where the cliff edge and a series of huge boulders appeared to offer a reasonably easy climb down to the lower rocky ledges on to which the waves could be heard perpetually pounding. Diana left the edge of the hole and walked towards the boulders. John went with her.

I looked at Alice. We were both standing a few feet from the edge and several yards apart. Taking great care I knelt down, then eased myself on to my front so that I could see right over the edge. Alice followed suit. As I looked down at the waves sloshing against the rocks more than a hundred feet below, I could feel my heart beating against the cropped turf. I looked at the sheer rock face on the far side of the hole dotted with patches of grass that clung to the most negligible of ledges, running on a diagonal towards the bottom. Halfway up, my eye was drawn to the down-turned bright-red beak of a blue-black bird bigger than a jackdaw but smaller than a crow that was perched on one of the ledges. I caught my breath and looked up at Alice to see if she had seen it. She was looking at me and her scarlet lips formed a curve, but you couldn't really call it a smile.

· THE OBSCURE BIRD ·

The obscure bird
Clamour'd the livelong night

William Shakespeare, Macbeth

It was late. Gwen spent ten minutes helping Andrew tidy up the kitchen and then put her arms out for a hug and said she was going up to bed.

'I won't be long,' Andrew said as he released her with a kiss.

Gwen smiled.

'Of course not,' she said.

It was a ritual. She knew it would be at least an hour, probably two, maybe more, before he joined her.

Outside, an owl hooted.

Andrew's eyes were dark behind the round lenses of his glasses, unfathomable.

He turned to the sink as she walked towards the door to the hall, where she stopped and looked back at him. With his hands resting on the edge of the basin he appeared to be staring out of the window into the garden, which was cloaked in darkness. She watched him for a moment before turning to go.

Gwen lay in bed thinking about Andrew, worrying. She remembered one night earlier in the week when she had got up to go to the bathroom. Andrew's side of the bed had been empty, cold. She had presumed him to be in his study, or downstairs, but when she had chanced to look out of the bathroom window she had seen him standing in the middle of the lawn, his pale round face upturned staring at the mature trees at the end of the garden. She remembered thinking that the right thing to do would be to go down and speak to him, perhaps gently guide him back into the house as you would a sleepwalker, but she had returned to bed instead and fallen back to sleep. When Gwen had woken in the morning, Andrew had been beside her as normal.

She heard him climbing the stairs and reached for the switch to turn her bedside light off. Lying in the darkness, she heard his carefully weighted footsteps approach their bedroom door, stop for a moment and then continue past. She heard him stop outside the baby's room, where he would be listening for the sound of Henry's breathing, and then continue on down the landing to his own study at the rear of the house. She heard the door click shut and imagined him sitting at his desk, raising the lid of the laptop and then staring alternately at the screen and out of the window. She had stood at his open door one night, watching him divert his attention from one to the other and back again, until he had caught sight of her reflection in the window and spun around on his chair, blushing. She had allowed her eyes to drop to his computer screen but instead of the lurid insult of pornography she had seen nothing more unsavoury than the boxy iconography common to social networking sites.

'You know, you really should get more sleep,' Gwen murmured in the morning as Andrew brought her a cup of tea.

'I know, but... you know,' he said.

'What?'

'The professorship thing. I might not get it anyway, but I certainly won't if I don't get these papers done.'

'Mmm.'

In the bathroom, Duffy the cat lay on her back on the mat. Legs extended at either end of her glossy black body, she looked like a giant skate egg case. Gwen tickled her tummy and Duffy's head darted forward to nibble at her wrist.

Gwen checked in the baby's room and then went downstairs. A floorboard creaked as she entered the kitchen. Andrew had paused in the act of emptying the dishwasher and was staring out of the window at the garden. She went up behind him and threaded her arms under his and held him tightly around the chest, resting her chin on his shoulder.

'There's nothing we can do,' Gwen said.

Andrew's head swivelled around on his neck.

'About Henry,' she said, pulling back.

'Oh,' he said. 'No. I know.'

They disengaged and Gwen watched Andrew's back as he continued to empty the dishwasher. His shoulders were tense, hunched up. When he had finished, he closed the door of the machine with a quiet snap.

'It's all going to go, you know. All that,' he said, looking out of the window again. 'Not our trees obviously, but everything beyond, in the old railway cutting.'

He turned to look at her. She didn't know what to say.

'I mean, I know it's a good thing,' he continued, 'extending the tram system, or at least I thought it would be, but now I'm not so sure. Not now I think of the ecological cost. All those trees. Countless nesting sites.'

She looked at him without speaking for a moment before saying, 'I've got to go to work.'

At the hospital, Gwen sat in the canteen with Angela.

'How's Henry?' asked Angela.

'We won't know for a while. Thanks for asking.'

'Fingers crossed, love.'

'Thanks.'

'What about Andrew?' she asked.

'He's under pressure at work. Going for a professorship.'

'Ooh, professor, eh?'

'Doesn't half make him sound wise.' Gwen thought for a moment. 'Andrew's changing, though,' she said. 'Whether in response to Henry or what, I don't know.'

'What do you mean?'

Gwen looked at the fine lines fanning out from the corners of Angela's eyes, which deepened as she smiled.

'I saw an exhibit in the Didsbury Arts Festival,' Gwen said. 'It was in that new food shop on Burton Road. There was a bamboo cage hanging from the ceiling with a tiny little screen in it playing a video of birds filmed in Beijing. Apparently, according to the artist's blurb – Daniel Staincliffe, his name was – old men meet up in the mornings to play chess all over Beijing and they take their songbirds with them in little cages. They hang the cages up in the branches of nearby trees and while the old men play chess the birds sing to one another.'

'Aah.'

'Yeah, cute, isn't it?' Gwen said. 'But it made me think of Andrew. He's like one of those birds stuck in his cage tweeting to other lonely people trapped in their own cages.'

'Tweeting?'

'You know, Twitter, Facebook.'

'Waste of time.'

'I know. Something's happening to him. He's changing. We hardly talk any more; we never have sex. I almost wish he'd raid the savings account and buy a sports car or have an affair.'

Angela laughed.

Gwen looked at her watch.

'Better get on,' she said.

Gwen was standing at the kitchen table checking through the post.

'Anything?' said a voice behind her.

'Christ!' She spun around. 'You made me jump. You creep around so bloody quietly these days.'

'Sorry.'

Duffy joined them in the kitchen.

'She's got something,' Andrew said, bending down.

Duffy opened her jaws and dropped a dead mouse on the wooden floor.

'Well done, Duffy,' Gwen said. 'That's a good girl.' She knelt down to tickle her and stroke her.

'You make more of a fuss of the cat than you do of me – *these days*,' Andrew said.

Gwen gave him a look and he smiled weakly.

'Sorry,' he said.

'What do you want to eat?' she asked him.

'I don't know.'

'Well, Duffy knows what she wants, don't you, Duffy?' she said, as if speaking to a baby.

The cat closed her nutcracker jaws around the mouse's head and bit down with a sustained audible crunch. They both watched as Duffy worked on the mouse, tearing at the skin and cracking its tiny bones. After a short while, the remains on the kitchen floor were no longer identifiable. Gwen wondered if Duffy would leave the guts and the legs and the tiny feet, but she swallowed every last shred, the bristly tail slipping down her throat last of all. Gwen realised she was grimacing; she felt a little sick. Previously when Duffy had brought in birds or mice, either Gwen or Andrew had taken them off her and, if they were still alive and not too badly damaged, freed them outside.

Knelt down next to Gwen, Andrew turned his head through ninety degrees to look directly at her. His black eyes were expressionless.

Gwen rose to her feet, knee joints popping. She went to the fridge and got out a plastic container of leftover homemade soup.

'We'll have this,' she said and pressed the button to open the door of the microwave. She gave a small cry and dropped the container of soup. It landed on its corner, dislodging the lid, and most of the soup splashed out on to her stockinged feet and on to the floor, quickly spreading.

'What the fuck is that?' she shouted, pointing inside the microwave.

'Ah, sorry,' Andrew answered, grabbing a roll of kitchen paper and a couple of tea towels, and mopping ineffectually at Gwen's feet. 'That's an owl pellet.'

'What the fuck is an owl pellet and what is it doing in the microwave?' she yelled.

'Owls regurgitate the parts of their prey they can't eat. Bones and fur and stuff. It all comes out in a little bundle, all carefully wrapped up like that. It's called an owl pellet.' As he explained, Andrew wiped the floor. He filled a bowl with soapy water and started scrubbing.

'Why is it in the microwave?'

'If you want to dissect one you should sterilise it first and the best way to do that is in the microwave. Otherwise the pellet can still be carrying rodent viruses or bacteria.'

'Jesus!'

Gwen left the room.

Dinner that night was a strained affair. Afterwards they sat at opposite ends of the sofa watching something on television that neither of them wanted to watch. As soon as it was over, Gwen announced she was going to bed.

'It'll give you a chance to dissect your owl pellet,' she said. 'Where did you get it, anyway?'

'In the cutting. I climbed over our back wall and had a bit of a look around. It's amazing. It's completely overgrown. There must be so much wildlife there that will all be left homeless when they clear everything for the tram tracks.'

'It was a railway line in the first place.'

'I know, but that was forty or fifty years ago and an entire ecology has grown up there since, and now that's going to be destroyed, for what? So that we can take the tram to Chorlton? No one's going to use it to go all the way into town. It's a long and roundabout route. It'll take forever and cost a fortune. They should have had the bottle to take it up Wilmslow Road and get rid of all those awful buses.'

She looked at him and shrugged her general agreement with his argument.

'I found the owl pellet at the base of one of the trees. There must have been an owl roosting there.'

'Right,' she said, softening. 'See you later. Will you look in on Henry?'

'Yes, of course. Goodnight.'

Gwen fell asleep straight away. Some time in the night, she was aware of the duvet being lifted on Andrew's side and cold air wafting over her arm. Then the draught was shut off and she felt the warmth of his body next to hers. As she started to drift back to sleep, she heard him softly speak.

'It's because of the serrations on my remiges.'

'What?' she said, confused, half-asleep.

'That's why I move so silently. From room to room.'

'Go to sleep, Andrew. Please.'

He fell silent.

Gwen woke again and felt anxiety's talons seize her immediately.

Andrew's side of the bed was cold, empty.

She got up and walked on to the landing. The darkness told her it was still night-time. She checked her watch; it was almost three. She opened the door to Henry's room. She saw his blue-and-white-striped babygro stretched out in the cot. Andrew was not in the room. The door to Andrew's study was open; he was not inside. Slowly she descended the staircase and turned left at the bottom to stand in the kitchen doorway. Andrew was standing in front of the sink staring out of the window. She took a step forwards and one of the wooden boards creaked. Andrew's head started to turn.

And continued to turn. It turned through ninety degrees and kept turning.

She stood absolutely still, scarcely breathing.

Andrew had not turned his body from the sink, but his gaze was now directed towards the fridge just to her left. Another few seconds and he would have twisted his neck through a hundred and eighty degrees.

Gwen felt the hairs on her arms rise. She backed out of the room and walked quickly but quietly upstairs.

She lay in bed and did not hear any movement from downstairs. At some point she fell asleep.

In the morning, making the bed, she found a feather on

the bottom sheet. She inspected the pillows and plumped them up.

Andrew was in the kitchen. They tiptoed around each other.

At work, Gwen logged out of the hospital intranet and on to the internet. She looked up 'remiges', trying various spellings until she found the right one.

'Tiny serrations on the leading edge of their remiges help owls to fly silently,' she read.

She decided they needed to talk.

When Gwen arrived home, the kitchen was in darkness, but the light at the top of the stairs was on. She hung up her coat and stowed her bag. She wondered about making a drink and waiting in the kitchen. At some point, he would have to come down. And she would ask him to explain himself.

Instead, she found herself walking up the stairs. She was halfway up when she heard him cough. He coughed again, abnormally, as if he was trying to clear his throat. Then there was a series of choking sounds. Her brother had once choked on a piece of meat when they were small and their mother had saved him by performing the Heimlich manoeuvre, sending a scrap of roast beef shooting out of his mouth, but it had been the choking sound that had stayed with Gwen. She was hearing it again now, a desperate, almost metallic squawking, mechanical and animalistic at the same time. She ran up the remaining stairs and stopped on the landing.

Andrew was standing in the middle of the bathroom, bent over at the waist. There was a small, indistinct bundle on the floor in front of him and a string of drool hanging from his mouth. The bundle – the pellet – was rounded, tapered at one end and bristly with hair. Under the brightness of the bathroom light, the whiteness of bone gleamed.

She turned away. On the floor outside the baby's room at the other end of the landing she saw something she thought she recognised. She took a step towards it.

Even in the half-light she could make out the blue and white stripes.

· JIZZ ·

A buzzard soaring above the south-west corner of the Ardèche that afternoon would have spotted three human figures walking along a road leading from a nearby town into the forested hills to the north. Each was pulling a wheeled suitcase and one – the only man in the group – had an animal in tow as well, a dog, too large for the buzzard to take.

Occasional cars passed the three as they became strung out along the road. The man with the dog brought up the rear, perhaps reflecting the difficulty of having to use both hands to control things that didn't want to be controlled.

The woman in the lead stopped at the point where a path led from the road up to the forested hillside. She waited for the other woman to draw level with her and they moved close to each other, then looked to see how far back the man was, before they headed up the path. Its narrowness forced them to revert to single file. Before they rounded the first bend, they looked back to see the man reach the start of the path and turn in. The path joined a track and the two women walked side by side for a while. A short distance from a cluster of buildings in a clearing in the forest, they stopped and waited for the man to catch up, then the three of them, and the dog, walked the last part of their journey as a group.

A man in chef's whites walked over from the pool to welcome them, leaving two women and a man stretched out on loungers and another man swimming lengths. Behind the pool, the gardens swept away in a series of descending terraces. From the woods on the other side of the valley a sharp report was heard, followed by a second.

Simon and Latifa turned to look and Yasmin tried on a look of disapproval.

'*Les chasseurs*,' said the man who now stood before them.

'What are they hunting?' asked Yasmin.

'Wild boar mostly.'

'Mostly?'

'One young fellow shoots birds.'

'What birds?' asked Latifa.

'Whatever he can find. Thrushes, starlings, buntings – even hoopoes. In fact, especially hoopoes. *Malheureusement.*'

'Eagles?' Yasmin said, looking up at the sky. 'I thought I saw one when we were on our way.'

'It could have been an eagle,' said the man, 'but more likely a buzzard. But, please, allow me to welcome you to the Ardèche. I am Patrice.'

Yasmin introduced herself and added, 'This is my husband, Simon, and sister, Latifa. We have a booking.'

'Your sister or his sister?' Patrice asked, flashing white teeth.

He and Yasmin both looked at Simon and Latifa, who could not have looked less like brother and sister, Simon with his long neck and long, slender body and noticeably short legs, which he tried and failed to disguise by wearing skinny jeans. He affected an ironic Mohican, dyed a dusky blond colour, and had small dark eyes. Latifa was, as she had been ever since they had left puberty, slimmer and curvier and browner than her elder sister, but they had the same chestnut eyes. Latifa's luxurious hair reached halfway down her back.

'Can't you tell?' said Yasmin.

Patrice laughed and handshakes were exchanged.

'And who is this?' asked Patrice, getting down to his haunches.

'This is Sonny,' said Simon.

'*Hé, qui c'est le gentil chien?*' Patrice petted the dog, talking as if to a small child. '*Mais tu es très beau, tu sais. Je suis sûr que tu vas te plaire ici.*' He returned to a standing position and switched back to English. 'Come. I will show you to your rooms. This,' he said, pointing to an elevated open-air terrace, 'is where we have dinner, every night except Sunday.'

Yasmin found herself walking beside Patrice, as he continued to point out features of the house and grounds, which meant that Simon and Latifa were left to fall in step behind them. The sounds of the swimmer working his way methodically up and down the pool faded as they stepped into the shadow of the house and outbuildings. Patrice stopped at a door.

'This is the double room,' he said, addressing Yasmin, 'for you and your husband. I presume,' he added, with a smile and a half-raised eyebrow, which Yasmin ignored. 'And the single room, for *mademoiselle*,' and here he smiled broadly in Latifa's direction, 'is at the top of the steps. The blue door. Dinner is at seven, but I invite you for drinks at six on the terrace.'

In the relative cool of the room, Yasmin set about unpacking. Simon's case stood by the door. He had unzipped it halfway just to take out and put on his Newcastle United shirt. The T-shirt he had travelled in was lying on the floor.

'I'll take Sonny out for a walk,' he said.

'We just walked from the town,' said Yasmin.

Simon remained standing for a moment, holding Sonny's lead and looking at the floor, then he opened the door.

When they had gone, Yasmin sat on the bed. She looked up at the wall. There was a framed watercolour, a forestscape. On the other side of the wall Latifa would be unpacking. Or showering after the journey. Having a lie-down.

There was a little bookcase under the window. Some crime novels, a bird book, a copy of Ovid's *Metamorphoses*. Yasmin lay back on the bed and curled up on her side. It would be her first and last chance to enjoy laundered sheets before Simon turned the bed into a foul-smelling nest.

The next thing she knew, there was crashing and banging and something heavy and smelly landed on top of her. Not Simon, but Sonny, licking her face. She fended him off.

'You know I don't like that,' she complained.

Simon ignored her and sat down on the end of the bed, where Yasmin had sat before lying down and falling asleep. She saw him looking at the bookcase. He took a book out, the bird book, and said, 'What the fuck?' and exploded into raucous laughter. 'Look at this,' he said, leaning back next to her. 'What the fuck? *Jizz!? Birds by Character: The Fieldguide to Jizz Identification.*'

Yasmin grabbed the pillow and placed it over her head.

'I was trying to sleep,' she said.

'Listen to this,' he said. 'This is the introduction. "The overriding purpose was to convey more fully than ever before the general *character* – or jizz – of most British and

European birds." Ha, get this. "Jizz is instantly appreciated, but its meaning is understood only through experience." Yasmin, are you listening?'

'Go away.'

The first guests to arrive on the terrace were the Belgian couple, Thomas and Marie. He was an accountant, she worked for the government. They were nice, quiet, no trouble. It was their second time. Patrice had all his bottles of homemade aperitifs lined up on the table. Thomas and Marie had been there a few days already, so there was no need for the routine. Marie chose the orange wine, Thomas the apricot.

Footsteps on the wooden stairs announced new arrivals. This would be the English party. The couple from Toulouse usually came through the house.

'*Bonsoir mesdames, bonsoir monsieur,*' Patrice said as the two Englishwomen – he assumed they were English, although they looked of Arab origin – reached the top step, the Englishman's extraordinary haircut bobbing into view behind them.

He gave the welcome speech, did the routine. The sisters both chose the orange wine and Simon the chestnut, as Patrice had known he would.

The Toulouse couple, Alain and Delphine, arrived and Patrice made the necessary introductions before slipping into the kitchen where he reminded Isabelle that Simon required kosher and Isabelle pointed out that she didn't need reminding.

'*C'est lui, avec les cheveux?*' she said.

'*Ben, oui, c'est lui,*' said Patrice with a shrug.

When Patrice returned to the terrace, Simon appeared

to be in the middle of telling a story and everyone else was listening politely, although he was speaking English and, as far as Patrice knew, neither the Belgians nor the French couple spoke the language.

'"—instantly appreciated,"' Simon was saying, loudly and with an exaggerated expression of disbelief on his face, '"but its meaning is understood only through experience."'

Patrice noted the blank looks on the faces of Alain and Delphine, and Thomas. Marie, however, was frowning.

'What is jizz?' she asked.

Simon pulled another face and sniggered and regarded his wife, who shook her head and looked at the floor, and then he turned to her sister, who was also shaking her head, but with a half-smile on her lips.

Patrice joined his fingertips together and announced that it was time to be seated. He saw Simon looking at the shared table and clearly wondering where his party's separate table was. *Tant pis! Tant pis pour tout le monde*.

As he served up the gazpacho with nasturtium leaf, Patrice reminded everyone that this was the final dinner of the week, Sunday being their night off. Dinner would resume on Monday. He saw Simon bristling, so he mentioned that there were restaurants in the town or they were welcome to enjoy a picnic, even a barbecue, in the grounds.

'More wine for you, *mademoiselle*?' Patrice said, carafe poised over Latifa's empty glass.

They left the dinner table as soon as they could.

'Whose idea was it to come here?' Simon asked as they made their way down the wooden steps from the terrace, the sounds of conversation fading behind them. 'As if I didn't know,' he added, with a look at Yasmin.

Yasmin shushed him. 'If we can hear them, they can hear us. Anyway, it was Latifa's idea, wasn't it?'

'I said we should go away together,' Latifa responded. 'I didn't pick this place. To be honest, I thought Simon did.' She looked at him. 'Did you have to go on about that bird book? It was so embarrassing.'

He returned the look. 'You know what, in some ways you're very different from Yasmin. In other ways you're just the same.'

He pushed open the door to the room and let it close behind him. Sonny, at least, was pleased to see him, jumping up and barking. He cuddled the dog for a bit, vaguely aware of the sound of Latifa's door opening and closing. Yasmin didn't appear; she would be hanging out with her sister, no doubt slagging him off.

'What do you reckon, buddy, make or break? This holiday. I think so, don't you?'

He undressed and got into bed. Five minutes later he got up and used the bathroom, then got back into bed. He held the covers up and spoke to the dog.

'Come here, Sonny. Come and get in here. Come on.'

Sonny stayed put, curled up on his improvised basket, some dirty washing that Simon had thrown in the corner.

'Suit yourself.'

Although it was warm, he pulled the thin quilt over his head out of habit.

He removed the quilt and reached for his bag, which he then dragged across the floor until it was by the side of the bed. From inside it he took a bottle of Scotch and unscrewed the cap. There wasn't much left. It wasn't worth saving. A couple of swigs. Another. And another. All gone. Back under the quilt.

He was drifting in and out of sleep, but was aware of the door opening. When Yasmin got into bed, Simon turned over so that he was facing her curved back. He slipped his arm around her waist and felt her tense up. He moved his hand further up her body and she shifted away from him. He withdrew his arm and turned over to face the other way. After a time, he pushed back the quilt and got out of bed. Sonny twitched in the corner, but then settled. Simon sat on the sofa and waited. Yasmin's breathing slowed to a steady rhythm. He switched on a lamp and looked at the bookcase again. He took out Ovid's *Metamorphoses*, flicked through it. He lifted it up to his nose. It smelt faintly of the past. He put it back and took out the bird book again. At first it made him smile, but then he felt the smile slide off his face. He put the bird book back and switched the lamp off. He sat there, listening to Yasmin breathe, then got up and opened the door. He slipped outside and closed the door behind him quietly. The night was still and warm. He turned and looked at the steps that led up to Latifa's room. The stone was cool under his bare feet.

When the knock came, she shrank back against the wall, her arms clasped around her knees. A second knock and then the handle turned, but the door was locked – now.

'Latifa.' It was her sister. 'Latifa, are you in there? Latifa.'

She moved across the floor on her hands and knees and unlocked the door.

Yasmin looked down at her.

'Latifa.'

She moved away and sat back against the wall again, adopting the same pose.

'Latifa, what's the matter?' Yasmin came in, leaving the door open.

Latifa looked at the door. Yasmin closed it.

'What's wrong, sis?' Yasmin crouched down opposite her, eyes wide.

Latifa allowed her head to drop.

'You didn't have that much to drink. We ate the same. OK, maybe you had a couple more glasses of wine, but I'm serious, *what is wrong with you?* Why won't you talk to me?'

Yasmin came and sat next to her and put her arm around her shoulder, but Latifa shrank away.

'What's the matter? Sis, *what's wrong?*'

Latifa stared at the tight skin on her knees.

'I don't know what's going on,' Yasmin said. 'Simon's disappeared—'

At the mention of his name, Latifa had winced.

'I haven't seen him all morning. He hasn't taken the dog for a walk. I know, because the dog is in our room. Probably needs to go out actually…' She fell silent and stared at the unmade bed. 'You haven't seen him?' she asked, redirecting her gaze at Latifa. 'Simon, I mean, not Sonny.'

Latifa looked down at her knees. She unclasped her arms and reached with her left hand for her phone, which was lying on the floor. She picked it up and opened her photos. She touched the last photo and handed the phone to Yasmin.

'What's this?' asked Yasmin, taking the phone from her and screwing her eyes up to look at the screen.

Latifa turned away.

'It's, what, a man in a doorway? Is it Simon?' She glanced at Latifa, whose attention was now on the door. 'In your doorway? You've got a photo of Simon standing in your doorway on your phone? What's going on, Latifa?'

Latifa looked at the phone in Yasmin's hand. The screen dimmed and Yasmin touched it with a finger. It wasn't a good picture. It was dark and it was blurred. The image was no better than a silhouette, but Yasmin had obviously recognised him, the long neck and long body. She was staring at Latifa now. Latifa gazed at the phone, which happened to grow dim again at that point. She reached across and touched the screen herself, then touched it again so that it showed what time the photo had been taken. After one in the morning.

Yasmin turned slowly to look at Latifa, who saw her sister's eyes narrow and a vertical furrow appear above the bridge of her nose. Two lines were drawn either side of her mouth as if she were about to speak, and she pulled her head back slightly, but then stopped. The lines didn't get any longer or deeper. Then her eyes widened a fraction and simultaneously the frown deepened and her head moved forward like a bird's. Yasmin put the phone down and placed her hand on Latifa's bare forearm and Latifa rested her own free hand on top of her sister's. Latifa held her gaze.

Yasmin's lips parted, a gossamer thread of saliva lengthening between them. 'Latifa,' she said, 'I'm so sorry.'

Latifa allowed herself to be embraced.

'I'm so sorry,' Yasmin kept on saying, her face buried in Latifa's hair. 'So, so sorry.'

Sonny was curled up in his corner. He pricked up his ears at a noise and opened his eyes, but the door didn't open. There was no change in the play of light in the room. He closed his eyes again. He saw paths, tracks, roads. He saw birds, toads, rabbits. He didn't see his master. He didn't see his master's women. He felt himself twitch and rearranged his limbs. He opened his eyes again and looked around the room. His master's bed. Bags, clothes. The bookcase, books.

Footsteps. The door opened. The women came in, shut the door. He barked. He saw paths, rabbits, tracks, hills, sky, trees, pine needles, scattering birds. He barked. His master's woman was holding something sharp and shiny. She handed it to the other woman and came towards him. She knelt down and cuddled him. She patted him, petted him. Her face was a mask. He barked. She gathered him up in her arms and carried him through into the bathroom. He barked. He barked. He barked.

Perhaps it wasn't the best time of day for hunting, but at least he would be unlikely to hit another hunter, orange hats or no orange hats. He didn't wear the orange hat himself. If he got hit, he got hit. He wouldn't get hit. Although, if he got hit, they would say he died doing what he enjoyed doing. It was how he would have wanted to go. That was what they would say.

He saw movement through the trees. A bird? A boar? He crept silently closer. He smelt smoke. Neither a bird nor a boar. It was a woman. And another woman. Two women, guests at Patrice's place, presumably. It looked like they had picked a spot right at the edge of his land, almost in the forest. They appeared to be preparing a picnic. More than a picnic. A feast. He settled himself behind a tree, where he could lean his body against the trunk and still see. Watch, if he was honest. He stood the stock of his rifle on the forest floor, rested the muzzle against the tree. He made himself comfortable.

They were dark, these women, like Arabs. Dark hair, dark eyes. But they were not covered up. The older woman wore a white T-shirt, the younger woman a brown top. As they continued to set up their feast, attending to the barbecue, arranging the pieces of cheese, the slices of cold meat, there were flashes of flesh that reminded him of a film he had seen years ago. It was a good memory, an exciting memory. He repositioned himself against the tree, opened his legs a little. He seemed to need more room. He put one hand in his pocket. One of the women turned the strips of meat on the barbecue. A rich, hot, smoky smell penetrated the tree line. He wondered if they would sit down, drink wine, start caressing each other, like in the film. But then they both turned and looked, off to their right, his left. Someone was coming. Another woman? His eye searched the climbing terraces for a figure descending. He spotted movement. A strange hairstyle, like a crest, but a man, in light-brown shorts and a black-and-white-striped shirt. The newcomer advanced towards the women, picking his way down the levels of the terraced hillside. The women both stood up straight, one, the younger-looking one, seeming to take up a position slightly behind the older one. The man stopped while still a little way off, as if unsure of his ground. The man was saying something. The women gestured at the feast. The man looked at the spread, then back at them. They moved slightly, as if to make room. There was room. The man walked forward, stood at one end of the blanket on which the food had been laid out.

He removed his hand from his pocket, touched the barrel of the gun for comfort. In a way he wished the man hadn't arrived, but it could still be good.

The women were saying something, gesturing. The man bent down, took a piece of cold meat, placed it in his mouth. The older woman pointed to the barbecue, exclaiming. He couldn't tell what they were saying, but they appeared to be encouraging the man to try something off the barbecue.

The younger woman produced a paper plate, passed it to the older woman, who picked up a couple of pieces of cooked meat from the barbecue and put them on it. She passed it to the man and then she poured him a plastic cup of wine and gave him that as well. The women stood and watched the man eat. He was nodding his strange, crested head as he ate, apparently enjoying the food. He looked at the spread, seeing what else there was. At the end nearer to where the women were standing was an inverted bowl. Maybe a tart or something, kept covered. The man pointed at it. The women looked at each other and the older woman bent down and lifted the bowl. What was underneath didn't immediately make sense. It wasn't a tart or a gateau or a flan or a crème caramel. It looked like one of the novelty cakes people sometimes had specially made for children's birthdays. This one was in the shape of the head of a dog.

The man dropped his plate. It turned in the air and landed upside down on the grass. There was a look of horror on his face. The two women's bodies looked suddenly tense, ready to flee. The man bent over, retching. The women watched in a sort of half-crouch as he slowly straightened again. The older woman picked up the dog's head and thrust it towards the man. Then she threw it so that it landed at his feet. She wiped her hand on her T-shirt, leaving a wide smear of blood. Then everything seemed to happen both very quickly and very slowly. The man started moving towards the two women, striding across the picnic blanket, his hands bunched into fists. The women turned as if to run, grim-faced. And then the man wasn't there any more and the women had disappeared. There was a hoopoe standing in the middle of the picnic and two other smaller birds in the air, one a small brown bird. It could have been anything, but it sang like a nightingale as it flew towards the tree line. The other small bird moved quickly on its long wings, darting this way, then that way, a short blue body, a flash of red on the breast, a swallow.

The hoopoe sensed movement in the trees and twisted its long neck. It spread its broad, barred wings and took flight, like a butterfly, but as the shot rang out the bird was caught, as if pinned to the air.

· STUFFED ·

I unlock the door to my flat and enter. It is warm and smells of books. I close the door and put my laptop bag down in the living room and my book bag on the kitchen table. Only when I have switched on the corner lamps in the living room and the under-cupboard lighting in the kitchen do I take the books out of the bag. The duster and polish are in the cupboard under the sink. Top of the pile is *Bethany* by Anita Mason, her first novel, published by Abacus in 1984. The first edition, I see from the imprint page, had been with Hamish Hamilton three years earlier. That would have been a hardback; I collect paperbacks. I point the nozzle of the spray can at the front cover and apply the duster. The spine has some faint staining that will not come off and on the back cover there is a Gift Aid sticker to be removed. Two more Abacus paperbacks follow, then a Paladin, two Sceptre titles and three Picadors, including Angela Carter's *Nights at the Circus*. If I show this to Jen, she will ask me if I haven't already got it. I'll say I have, but with a different cover.

I interrupt the cleaning of the books to go to the Picador shelves in the hall and take down my other copy of *Nights at the Circus* with its jauntier, more playful cover illustration by Jean-Christian Knaff (or Jean Christian Knaff, as the credit line has it). I prefer the softer, more mysterious image on the copy I have just bought, by Louise Brierley, plus I already have a Picador edition of Carter's *Love*, also with a Louise Brierley cover: a couple in bed, asleep, and a fox on a little table that could be either frozen in a block of ice or stuffed in a glass case.

When I have cleaned them all, I straighten the pile of new acquisitions and sit looking at them for a while. They are all the same size – B-format – and all have white spines. I take the Angela Carter, Robyn Davidson's *Tracks* and Rudolph Wurlitzer's *Slow Fade* and shelve them with the Picadors. The Abacus, Sceptre and Paladin titles I take to their respective bookcases, which are, like the Picador shelves, white and of uniform design.

I return to the kitchen to make a cup of tea and while I am standing waiting for the kettle to boil I look out of the window at the flat directly across the courtyard, which, on the outside, and structurally, is a twin of my flat. It had been empty for a while but recently acquired a new resident, a man in early middle age, like me, but, unlike me, with a full head of hair. The lights are on in his bathroom and I can make out the shape of his dark head bobbing around behind the frosted glass. It looks as if he is washing his hands or cleaning his teeth.

I lie in bed, trying to sleep, under the glassy gaze of my jay, which stands guard, on its polystyrene rock, on the bookcase in the bedroom that is filled with A-format Penguins with their orange spines, author name in black, and white title. I am reminded, as I am every time I look at my books, of the piece written about me and my collection in a Sunday supplement that used the term 'colour coding' and prompted a number of tagged photographs on social media of chaotic bookshelves of rainbow hues, books of all sizes standing incongruously next to each other.

In the morning, waiting once more for the kettle to boil, I look across the courtyard. The man in the flat opposite is either a different man – and bald – or it's the same man and he's shaved his head. I realise I'm running my hand over my own shorn scalp as I watch him.

Jen is coming up today. She will stand in the living room of my flat. She will look at the owl on the bookcase in the corner, which she bought me – the owl, not the bookcase – and say, 'You like our owl?' And I will say, 'It's artificial?' And she will answer, 'Of course it is.' Every relationship has its habits and routines.

The kettle clicks off. I warm the pot and make my tea.

When I get back from work, Jen is already there, sitting on the sofa, her blonde hair turned platinum in the glow of her laptop. I enter the living room and look at the owl. She looks at the owl and delivers the line. I respond and she responds to my response.

While I am cooking dinner, I glance out of the window. I see the man in the flat opposite attempting to assemble a piece of flat-pack furniture in his living room. It looks like a white bookcase.

Jen tells me she is going out to the shop. Is there anything I want? I tell her it's not essential, but some basil would go nicely with the pasta I'm preparing. I watch the man wrestling with the long, white side pieces of his bookcase. Jen comes back with a bottle of wine and a basil plant in a pot. I put the basil on the window ledge.

Later, we lie in bed looking at the jay.

'Oh, I nearly forgot,' Jen says, having picked up her handbag to look for her phone. 'I got you a present.'

She hands me a white-spined Picador. Tom Wolfe's *The Bonfire of the Vanities*.

'To go with your white books,' she says. 'I hope you haven't already got it.'

'Not this size,' I say, handling it gingerly until I can clean it and give it back to Oxfam.

'There are different sizes?' she asks.

'They did a handful of titles in A-format.'

'They must be very collectable,' she says in a neutral tone.

'They were intended for cover-mounts,' I say. 'Given away with *GQ*. That sort of thing.'

In the morning there is a pot plant on the kitchen window ledge across the way. From this distance I can't identify it with the naked eye. Even without my binoculars – on special offer from the RSPB – I can see that there are already some books on the man's newly constructed bookcase in his living room. I can't see the names of their authors, or identify their publishers, but they have white spines.

It is a simplification – and inaccurate – to say that my collection is colour-coded. If Chekhov's stories are shelved separately from Katherine Mansfield's, the distinction is not between black and pale green, but between Penguin Classics and Penguin Modern Classics.

If I stand at one of the windows on the other side of my flat, where the view is on to the communal gardens, I often see one of a pair of resident jays, sometimes both of them. I tend to notice one only when it flies from one branch to another, displaying its white rump, and its mate will only become apparent when it, too, takes to the wing.

Jen leaves, saying she will be back at the weekend. I go to work and visit the charity shops in town on my lunch hour, but their stock takes some time to be refreshed. Nevertheless, I return home with a Picador edition of Keri Hulme's

The Bone People, cover by Robert Mason, withdrawn from Gloucester County Library. While I am reaching under the sink for the polish and duster I notice all the lights are on in the flat across the courtyard. I see no sign of the man in any of his windows, but then I hear the boot of a car being slammed shut and look down into the courtyard to see the man walking towards the exterior stairs at the back of his block of flats carrying a pile of books. He walks up the three flights of stairs and knocks on the back door to his kitchen. From the hall, a blonde woman enters the kitchen and opens the back door. Together they move into the living room and she holds the pile of books while he takes them from her one at a time to put them in their correct places on the shelves. I get my binoculars from the cupboard to confirm that he is shelving the books – Picadors – alphabetically and that the woman helping him is Jen.

When he has finished, he takes a step back to admire his handiwork. Jen steps back also and it is only at this point, as the focus widens, that I see the stuffed owl sitting on another bookcase at the far end of the room. The man appears to be staring in that direction. Jen follows his gaze. I am about to lower the binoculars when the owl appears to move. It dips its body slightly and then spreads its wings and launches itself from its perch. I imagine I can hear the rustling of its feathers as it flies the short distance across the room and lands on the white bookcase. Jen is looking, not at the owl, but at the man. I see her lips move. The man turns to look at her and then looks back at the owl, which turns its head to look at him. He then turns back to Jen and I see his lips move, too, and then Jen's, again.

· PINK ·

Geoff stood motionless among the trees watching a stocky buff-coloured bird with a sky-blue bar on its wing. The jay was perched on a branch twenty feet above his head. Geoff had been watching it for five minutes, maybe ten. You lost track of time. You went out for a short walk and came home two hours later. The soft rubber grip of the binoculars sat comfortably in his hands. The jay twitched, flicked its tail. Still Geoff watched it.

The jay hopped on to a higher branch and Geoff followed it with his binoculars. Every jay was interesting. You might be thrilled to see one in the morning and just as excited to spot one in the afternoon.

It flew higher still and then switched to the next tree and became harder to see clearly against the light. Geoff breathed out as he lowered his binoculars. He rejoined the path, listening to the calls of various birds and their different patterns of song.

He saw the outline of a sparrow-sized bird on a leafless branch and raised the glasses again. A robin. He watched its reddish throat vibrate as it whistled and trilled. On his way out of the woods, he saw blue tits, goldfinches, two crows, a wren and, at the top of a Scots pine, a chaffinch giving voice to its warbling song.

He still hadn't seen a bullfinch.

There were lots of British birds that Geoff had never seen. What was special about the bullfinch? Avocet, bittern, corncrake – he could probably go right through the alphabet naming birds that weren't ticked off in his little book. But, for some reason, the bullfinch had always held a particular fascination for him.

It's rare, he told his colleague, Safraz, on the news desk.

Not as rare as the black redstart, Safraz retorted.

OK, but it has rarity value within its class, he said. It's the least common of our finches. Anyway, what do you know about the black redstart?

We ran a news story about it last summer, don't you remember? There was a pair of them nesting in town.

That had been before Geoff had got his binoculars, before his hobby had really taken off. He'd always been interested in birds, always enjoyed looking through his bird books, feeling strangely drawn into the idealised landscapes of the soft-hued illustrations in the older volumes. He'd pencilled discreet ticks on the pages of one particular book. And among the pages given over to finches there had remained one, over the years, unticked. That pink puffed-out chest, the thick blunt wedge of a bill, the inky-black head. His sister, Deborah, had recently moved to the country and reported on the variety of species that visited her garden.

Goldfinches, woodpeckers, bullfinches, a buzzard.

Bullfinches?

Yes, they come for the buds on the cherry tree.

Bullfinches, really?

Yes.

No.

Yes!

Geoff had bought the binoculars after his marriage

had finally fallen apart. They had been his consolation. Unable to see any reason for happiness or contentment close at hand, he had thought maybe if he could extend the range of his vision, things might not look quite so bleak. The purchase coincided with the first breath of spring. The birds singing in the trees were easily seen, not yet concealed by foliage, so he trained his binoculars in the direction of each new burst of song coming from the back garden. That lively twittering from the top of the laburnum – a goldfinch. A hurried warbling concluded by flute-like whistling from the privet – most likely the blackcap he had briefly glimpsed for the first time the previous afternoon. The call-and-response *schackachack schackachack* from within the overblown confection of gnarled twiglets and pink tissue-paper clumps that was the cherry tree – a stand-off between magpies.

The phone rang.

May I speak with Mrs Armitage?

Mrs Armitage is not here.

When will she be back?

She won't. Mrs Armitage is not coming back.

Geoff replaced the receiver and looked out of the window. A pair of coal tits that he had seen nesting in a hole in the wall of the house were now flitting around the bird feeder dangling from the cherry tree. Perched on the rim of the chimney pot of the house immediately behind Geoff's was a sleek, black crow.

Geoff collected his binoculars. The front door closed behind him. He didn't bother to double-lock it. He walked through the park, down the hill past the allotments, climbed on to the embankment above the river and headed upstream. Joggers, dog walkers and a couple holding hands went past him in the opposite direction. He stopped to watch a heron on the far bank. It stood on one leg, still as a sentry, staring at the water, its neck held in a tight S-shape. As he watched the bird through the glasses, he slowly raised his left foot behind him until his knee was bent at ninety degrees. When the heron finally moved it did so with such extreme slowness Geoff was oblivious until he realised the tight S had been extended by six inches or so. It had moved with the stealth of a minute hand. Geoff lowered his left leg and took several careful steps, giving the circulation a chance to return to his foot before trusting it again with his weight.

Geoff stopped at the end of a long straight section. He looked across the river. On the far side, a golfer took a swing and a ball flew up from the grass at his feet. A split-second later came the *pock* of wood on hard rubber. The golf ball had not yet reached the vertex of its trajectory when Geoff turned and walked down the embankment away from the river. A small bird called from a tree at the end of two long lines of poplars either side of the main path. A chiffchaff.

Geoff crossed the path and cut through a small section of woodland. A torn scrap of newsprint caught his eye and he thought of Safraz. Standing at the edge of the woodland he looked out at a broad field in front of him. Widely dispersed clumps of dry reedy grasses, small birds, brown, white and black, clinging to hollow stems – reed buntings, he saw, when he raised the glasses. At the far side of the field was a line of trees, a copse flattened by perspective. A hawthorn in flower, a hornbeam, ash. Geoff heard a quiet piping call and made out a bird perched on a branch towards the crown of the nearest tree. He squinted through the binoculars. A chaffinch? Another reed bunting? He didn't think so. He needed to get closer. Slowly he started to cross the field, not taking his eyes off the bird in the tree; its colours were wrong, too vivid and too dark at the same time. He knew if he stopped to raise the glasses it would be in that instant of unseeing that the bird would fly away. He couldn't miss this, in case, *in case*... He did stop and he knelt down and then as inconspicuously as possible he lifted the binoculars. The glossy black head and plump salmon-pink chest. The grey and black back and wings. The blunt, bulbous beak. The bullfinch.

He watched it with steady hand for a minute or more until it stepped off the branch and flew towards him. He lowered the glasses and as they came to rest against his chest he could feel the thump of his heart. The bullfinch flew over his head and back the way he had come, towards the woodland, where it disappeared among the trees.

He walked home with his chest puffed up like that of the bullfinch.

He had tried sleeping on her side of the bed, but it wasn't right. It didn't work and merely emphasised her absence. Now, sleep came easily. He made sure of it by not coming to bed until he was too tired to remain awake. In the mornings, he woke slowly to the sound of birdsong, clinging to his dreams until consciousness reminded him of what he had sought to forget. But the morning after he had seen the bullfinch, he felt happy. He pictured it all pink and black on its branch, its piping voice drowning out the birds outside his window. The budding foliage around it and the nearby trees all in soft focus. The light striking its prominent chest.

Geoff stretched his calf muscles and rotated his ankles before getting out of bed. He pulled back the curtains and there in the tree outside his window was a suddenly familiar bird with a pink chest, jet-black cap and wings of steel grey.

The bullfinch sat on the branch staring not at him, but in his direction, straight at the window, into the house. Geoff backed away.

He entered the bathroom and regarded himself in the mirror. He looked haunted. He cleaned his teeth, splashed water on his face, then went to open the blind. A bullfinch sat at the top of the laburnum, quietly issuing a single repeated note. Another clung to the bird feeder, hanging upside down like a long-tailed tit. A third bullfinch hopped across the lawn in the manner of a blackbird or a thrush.

Perched on the chimney pot of the house behind Geoff's was not a crow or a starling, but a bullfinch.

He returned to his bedroom. As he pulled on his socks, gooseflesh tingled and Geoff felt hot and cold at the same time. In the kitchen, he ate his breakfast with his back to the window. He stood at the sink with his empty bowl and looked up. There were now three bullfinches flitting about the bird feeder. The bowl fell into the enamel sink with a clatter and broke in half.

He picked up his binoculars and left the house.

As Geoff approached the end of the street, a bird flew out of a hedge and sought shelter in the low branches of a horse chestnut. Geoff saw a flash of pink and a dazzling white rump as it disappeared. In the park there were bullfinches issuing their melancholy *peu peu* call from the cherry trees and flying between the tall cypresses. He passed the allotments, fingering his phone, thinking about calling Safraz. But what would he say? How would it sound? Maybe he should text his sister, let her know he had finally seen a bullfinch. And another and another.

He climbed the embankment. There were no ducks on the river, only bullfinches flying across from one bank to the other. Instead of a heron standing guard, a lone bullfinch stood proud. He walked down the long straight section of the path by the river, speeding up. He saw no chiffchaffs, goldfinches, magpies, crows or blue tits. He listened but failed to hear the reassuring cooing of wood pigeons. All he heard was a faint piping warble, steadily increasing in volume. He ran across the path bordered by poplars and through the little patch of woodland. When he reached the edge of the field he stopped. There were no reed buntings clinging to the tall dry stalks – only bullfinches. Everywhere he saw the proud pink chest thrust out beneath the coal-black face. The copse at the far side of the field did not contain a flowering cherry, but its palette was dominated by a single colour.

As Geoff stood at the edge of the field, frightened to advance, scared to go back, he realised he had not seen a soul since waking up that morning. None of his neighbours had been out on the street. The park had been empty. On the road leading to the allotment no traffic had been moving. By the river he had not seen a jogger, a dog walker, a couple holding hands. He had neither seen nor heard anybody playing golf.

He reached into his pocket for his phone.

There was no signal.

The thin, hollow piping was getting louder and louder.

· THE BEE-EATER ·

You had been away just two days and I was woken early by birds outside our window. They sounded as though they were inside my head. Coiled tendrils of song slicing into my dreams like tapeworms through gut, but shiny, silvery, short and sharp like a stitching needle. My first thought, on becoming fully conscious, was one of grateful relief that I still had not had to go during the night. Even at that moment, as I moved on unsteady legs to the window, I could hang on. This was normal. Normal was good.

The tree was bare but for black clusters of seed pods that had attracted what seemed like dozens of tiny long-tailed birds all moving at once in different directions. It was like watching white noise or a stereogram that wouldn't settle. As I focused, the picture resolved itself into one that made sense. There were no more than five or six birds, but their jerky, acrobatic movements, now this way up, now that, suggested a greater number. One of them had a shorter tail. But if they were long-tailed tits, as I now realised they were, how could one have a shorter tail?

I spent the morning pretending to work, but all I was aware of was the constant need to visit the bathroom. I clung to one thing the doctor had said at my last appointment, that it was fantastically reassuring that I hadn't had to go during the night. And it was true, I hadn't.

In the afternoon I went to put the recycling bins out and

Jon, from across the street, happened to be out there doing his at the same time. His silver hair shone in the winter sunlight. You know me: I always have to have something to say. It's not enough just to nod and smile. So I told him about the birds that had woken me, because Jon knows his birds. I told him they were long-tailed tits but that one of them had a short tail. Did it have roughly similar colouring, he asked? Pretty much, I said. And he told me it must have been a coal tit, because coal tits are sociable and like to hang out with flocks of long-tailed tits.

I told Jon I reckoned I hadn't seen a coal tit for about 30 years. Or not knowingly.

It's a widespread species, he said with a smile. Often visits parks and gardens outside the breeding season.

Long-tailed tits too, I asked?

Widespread also, Jon said, if you discount Shetland, the Orkneys and the Outer Hebrides.

Jon smiled again and said that he and Megan were looking forward to coming over for dinner the following day. Me too, I said. You'd be home in time for that. You'd planned it, after all.

That night – last night – I went to bed late. I suppose I was thinking that if I stayed up till 2am and got up at eight, I'd make it less likely that I'd need to go during the night. As if by engineering the absence of symptoms, I could convince myself there was no disease. I dreamt, but when I woke at 6.15 I did not remember my dreams, because I was aware of one thing only, that I needed to go. It was a good hour and a half before my normal getting-up time.

So I tried lying there and not going. I tried thinking my way back into my dreams, back into sleep, but it didn't work. My breathing became faster, shallower. I noted that I had been sweating in the night. My father had suffered from night sweats in his final months. I told myself that I was the wrong age. I reminded myself that I'd had a good PSA result. But I also reran what the doctor had said, that it was fantastically reassuring that I hadn't had to go in the night. The logical corollary of that was that it was fantastically unreassuring that I did now need to go and since it was dark outside, although technically morning, it felt pretty much like the middle of the night to me. You were away; I was alone. I knew I would never get back to sleep.

I also knew that unless I managed to get an emergency appointment to see the doctor, the day would be lost to anxiety and panic.

The phone lines open at eight and are invariably engaged from that moment. I kept trying. I got the kids up and didn't tell them what was going on. I mustn't infect them with my worry, my phobia: behaviour learnt from my dad that I must not pass on to them. You're very clear about this and I agree with you. It's a curse. It's hard for you, I know it is. Your reassurance, since you are a doctor yourself, should be all I need, yet it's not. So I insult you twice. As my wife and as a doctor you are made to feel inadequate.

I got through. Could I make it for ten past eight, the receptionist asked? Otherwise there was nothing today. I left the kids. They could manage. (Unlike me.) It's only at the end of the road. My breath froze as it left my mouth. The skin on my hands dried and lost colour. I sat in the waiting room unable to do anything other than wait. I was an armed device. I heard my name over the tannoy.

In the consultation room, my words came out in a rush, tumbling over each other in the white water of my anxiety. My eyes switched between the doctor's face and a blurry photograph, a holiday snap, pinned to the wall. A brightly coloured bird. Jon would have known what it was from the colours alone. Orange, green, yellow, a line of black across the eye.

The doctor's hands alighted on his keyboard. He was saying that although he could treat the symptoms he'd rather not fill me full of drugs. At least not those drugs.

I said that was fine, as the symptoms themselves don't bother me. It's what they might signify. My breathing was getting faster.

I'd rather treat your anxiety than your symptoms, he said. Have you ever taken beta blockers?

My heart thumped. I'd never taken beta blockers, and whereas I didn't mind giving them a try, I knew they wouldn't be enough. I wanted to ask him to examine me, because I know you can have a good PSA result and it be misleading. You can still have the disease. But I couldn't ask him. It was too much, it was too degrading, for him and for me. But what else would reassure me? I perched on the edge of asking him to do it and I realised I was losing it. I'd started crying. Now at least it was easier to ask. So, I'm sorry, I said, and I asked and he said of course he'd examine me and he was on his feet walking towards the bed at the back of the room. He pulled the curtain for me to undress and lie down facing the wall. I felt nothing except fear. He told me to relax and strangely I found I almost could.

The healthy prostate should be smooth, he told me, like a plum, while a malignant prostate is gnarled like a walnut.

I felt a burrowing, an intrusion, yet no pain, little discomfort. Something turned inside me. I pictured the photograph stuck to the wall. Your prostate is extremely small, the doctor was telling me, and as smooth as a baby's bottom. Then he was gone, beyond the curtain. The snap of rubber, the splash of a running tap.

I sat down again and apologised once more.

The day can only get better, he said with a smile.

As I drive to the airport to pick you up I watch the planes gliding in like swans, herons, geese. I made a start on the beta blockers although I didn't really need to. Once the examination had been performed, my mind had been set at ease. My breathing had slowed, heart relaxed. I won't need to tell you anything of this. I feel a sense of satisfaction at having dealt with it myself this time. Of course, there'll be a next time. There always is. But we can concentrate on preparing for dinner tonight. I want to hear about your conference, your taste of the sun in the middle of our winter.

The symptoms persist, but once I know they're not sinister I don't care. You need to go more often, the doctor had said, just go. No big deal. I can still feel the ghost of a sensation, as if there's something there. The burrowing. My heart flutters at the memory of it.

You get dressed up, made up. Turquoise bracelet, abalone pendant, peacock shimmer. You look excited, beautiful. We switch the fairy lights on. People start to arrive for dinner. Connie and Bill, Annette and Paul, Jon and Megan. We've been sitting down only five minutes – pasta with green sauce and quail's eggs – when the coughing starts. A tickling in the throat. I move back slightly from the table as everyone turns to see if I'm all right, then I double up, retching. There's something inside me that shouldn't be. Choking sounds crackle from my throat. Eyes widen, mouths fall open. I hear my name being spoken. My shoulders hunch up, my neck contracts and something jerks up into my throat, shooting into my mouth and out on to the plate in front of me, a slithery bundle of bright colours. Orange, green, yellow. A black band, a curve and a sharp point.

Good God, cries Jon as everyone else backs away, chair legs squealing against the wooden floor. I can see in his face that while he's as shocked as the others, he's also detached. He's identifying the bird. He knows what it is.

You're looking at me in horror. I see tears spring to your eyes. You don't understand what's happening to me, and it distances you from me.

Do you know what that is, Jon asks in disbelief?

I think I do, I say.

Our only burrowing bird, he says in a strangely high-pitched voice. An occasional visitor, but only in the south. And never in the middle of winter.

Some people look at Jon and then at me, but after a moment all attention is focused back on the vividly coloured bird on my plate, struggling to open its wings, its black eye drawing our gaze.

· GANNETS ·

The island, which extended four miles out into the Atlantic, was connected to the tip of the peninsula by a cable car. The tide surged through Dursey Sound and a powerful wind ripped the tops off the waves. Claire held tight to Steve as the old car swung on the wire like overripe fruit. She couldn't help but compare Steve to her husband Victor. Steve was younger and more interesting, and moreover he was interested in her, attracted to her. They had been seeing each other for a few months; the trip to the west of Ireland was the most adventurous they had been so far. Victor thought she was birdwatching. Which she was.

'Look,' she said to Steve, pointing at a large black bird flying just above the water.

'What's that?' he asked.

'It's either a cormorant or a shag,' she said, smiling.

'Really?' he said, mindful of the tourists packed into the six-man car alongside them.

She squeezed his hand.

'Sorry to disappoint you,' she said, 'but it looks big enough to be a cormorant.'

The car lurched as it passed the second iron stanchion. Claire fell against the door, which slid open half an inch before Steve grabbed her. They exchanged a look as the car began its rumbling descent into the lee of the island.

A week or so later, Claire sat on a low wall across the street from the Godlee Observatory. Manchester's rush-hour traffic ground past, but she remained oblivious, her head full of memories. Ravens circling, soaring like eagles then flipping on to their backs and tumbling out of sight. The traditional music session, the thump of the bodhran like a heartbeat – faster, faster. Claire raised her gaze to the octagonal turret on top of the university's Sackville Street building. Squeezed out of the intricate architecture of the turret, the softer, more organic dimensions of the observatory's off-white dome reminded her of the sea anemones she and Steve had seen in the rock pools at Coonanna harbour.

Steve would be up there, with Victor, and the rest of them. They would have gathered in the Octagon Room beneath the observatory to swop notes on whatever private observations they had made since the last meeting. Each member of the society had their own optical instruments at home. None was anything like the size of the eight-inch refracting telescope in the observatory, of course, but a miniature version of the same. Victor had tried to explain why it didn't matter that the image was inverted, but she knew that if she looked through a telescope and saw a magpie hanging upside down from a branch like a sloth, it wouldn't do. So why were they happy to view the moon upside down, or to see the Great Red Spot *above* Jupiter's equator rather than *below* it? Or was it vice versa? Claire had never shared her husband's obsession with the stars. He had told her, before they had married, that it was a selfish hobby, because only one person could look through a telescope at a time, but he had never felt the need to apologise for this. Steve, whom she had first set eyes on across the Octagon Room at a Christmas party, seemed as interested as she was in the birds she watched through her binoculars. And so she started to show more of an interest in stargazing and would occasionally go along to meetings.

She went up in the lift to floor G.

'Hello, my dear,' Victor greeted her.

How absurdly old-fashioned he seemed, even for someone ten years her senior, especially under public observation. She understood. A certain pride attached itself to ownership. She had noticed the way some of the members looked at her.

'We were just saying,' remarked a man in a green fleece, 'that it's only another week until the conjunction.'

'The conjunction?'

'The conjunction of Venus and Saturn on the twenty-sixth and twenty-seventh,' said a man with a ponytail, his eyes shining. 'Both planets will be visible above the eastern horizon from an hour before dawn. They'll appear very close to each other, but of course are millions of miles apart.'

There followed a discussion as to whether it was preferable to observe the conjunction privately at home or to make the journey in the early hours to the observatory.

Claire, meanwhile, wondered why Steve was not in the room.

A few weeks after the Christmas party, Steve had tracked down Claire online, and soon their emails fell into a kind of relaxed flirtatiousness. They started meeting in the observatory, picking times when no one was likely to be there.

One night, they stepped out on to the viewing platform that ran around the outside of the dome.

'I like our private observations,' she said.

'They don't always seem to bring you much happiness.'

'You know why. It's nothing to do with you.'

'Where does he think you are tonight?'

'He's stopped asking.'

'Do you think he knows?'

'I don't know. But I do know he won't ever let me go.' Claire switched her gaze from the warmth of the city lights to the stars, which shone with a cold brilliance. 'When there's nothing to look at through his telescope, he follows me round from room to room.'

'Do you think you could ever leave him?' asked Steve.

'He tried to kill himself once,' she said quietly. 'I found him face down on the lawn – next to his telescope.'

'Why?'

'I asked him, when he got out of hospital, and all he said at first was, "There's nothing out there."'

'Meaning?'

'Out there.' She gestured at the heavens. 'I told him, "It's down here that matters," and he said there was nothing down here either, for him, apart from me. He made me promise then that I'd never leave him.'

On Dursey Island, having disembarked from the cable car, Steve and Claire climbed to the top of the nearest hill. Sheep ran through narrow gullies between clumps of heather and gorse. At the top, Claire collapsed on to the ground, Steve beside her.

'You seem so happy,' he said. 'So much more relaxed.'

'I hate all the deceit,' she said. 'And I hate that we can't spend proper time together. Out here it all seems so much simpler. I can see things more clearly.'

They walked towards the edge. The ground sloped away. Further down were steep cliffs. Claire asked Steve to pass her the binoculars.

'Do you think that door would have opened all the way?'

she asked as she watched a large white sea bird soaring above the water. 'On the cable car.'

'Maybe. I read the sign on the mainland. It's nearly forty years old.'

'If you fell out, you'd know about it,' she said, still watching the birds.

'If the fall didn't kill you, the tidal race would.'

'Gannets,' Claire said, passing the binoculars to Steve. 'Our biggest sea bird. Look! All-white body, black wing tips, yellow head. Unmistakeable – and so beautiful! If you keep watching you'll see one dive. They stop, fold their wings into their body and drop into the sea like a stone.'

They sat down on a ledge to watch the gannets, passing the binoculars between them. Claire noticed that when she was looking through them at the birds dive-bombing the ocean, the cliff edge in the foreground looked very close, as if it were a grassy bluff no more than a few feet away, and it was only when she lowered the glasses that she appreciated the danger.

'It's the foreshortening,' explained Steve. 'You're not aware of it looking through a telescope at the moon, because there's nothing in the foreground.'

Claire assessed what would happen if someone were to slip off the ledge on which they were sitting, thinking the grassy bluff to be beneath their feet. They'd fall and slide and be unable to stop before reaching the edge of the cliff.

She took up the glasses again and observed the gannets, the way they patrolled the waves, watching and waiting, before, in an instant, taking action. They would disappear beneath the surface and a few seconds would pass before they emerged several feet away.

'I can't carry on leading this double life,' she said as they walked back down the hill to the cable car. 'I need to take action.'

'I don't want to tell you what to do,' Steve said, taking her hand, 'but if you decide you want to be with me, I won't let you down.'

At the observatory, Claire followed Victor up the spiral staircase. As she climbed she remembered the advice Steve had given her the first time she had been in the observatory alone with him: 'Just keep turning to the left,' he'd said. Through the tall windows she looked out over the centre of town and wondered how out of all the myriad possibilities the city presented, her life had come to be inextricably tied to this one location.

She reached the top and stepped inside the observatory.

Claire had seen Steve and Victor standing close together before, but only in the high-ceilinged Octagon Room. Under the sloping roof of the observatory dome and crowded by the two big telescopes, their proximity to one another – Victor on the left, Steve on the right – was strangely disturbing. She remembered what the man with the ponytail had said about Venus and Saturn appearing close to each other but actually being millions of miles apart.

'I feel a bit faint,' she said.

For all the hours he spent gazing at distant worlds, Victor was a reluctant traveller. Claire, however, was determined to persuade him to go with her on what would be another trip for her to the west of Ireland.

'After the conjunction,' he finally agreed.

'No. It can't wait. I want to show you the gannets. They'll be flying south very soon.'

She pictured the ledge where she had sat with Steve. She remembered the effect of the foreshortening.

Victor pulled a face.

'It's important to me,' she pressed. 'I checked the long-range forecast. It's much better there. Stay here and you'll not see anything.'

On the cable car, she made sure that she and Victor were the last ones in, so they had to sit by the sliding door. She watched the narrow gap at the edge of the door. If Victor were to fall against it as she had done…

Was she really such a bad person? She would never consider killing another human being; failing to prevent an accident was hardly the same thing. Victor was unhappy. It would be a release.

On the island, the gannets had not flown south. Some of the non-breeding birds would remain all year round, but Victor would not have known that. It was easy to find the same ledge. Through the binoculars, the birds could be observed soaring and diving. The foreshortening pulled the grassy bluff closer until it appeared to be underfoot. All it would take would be for him to slip off the ledge…

Later, Claire stood in the chill pre-dawn air.

The French windows in the bedroom of the rented cottage back on the peninsula opened directly on to a small lawn at the bottom of which was a low fence. Just above the horizon was the planet Venus, shining bright as a searchlight. When Claire lifted her binoculars she could see a faint body slightly above and to the right of Venus. Although her glasses were not powerful enough to show its rings, she knew this was Saturn.

She stood and watched the planets. Venus on the left, Saturn on the right. As the darkness faded, it became harder to see them, although both planets did remain visible. The sun rose above the horizon and in a short while Venus was still relatively bright but Saturn had become much fainter.

Claire took out her phone and dialled a number.

'Are you at the observatory?' she asked.

'Yes,' said Steve.

'What's the weather like there?' she asked.

'Stormy. Raining and blowing a gale.'

'So no view of the conjunction?'

'None at all.'

'Why did you go in, then, rather than stay at home?'

'I knew there'd be no one else here. I wanted to be reminded of you.'

She paused, then said: 'It's over, Steve. Finished. I'm sorry. I've got to go.'

'Wait!' he said, but then fell silent.

'I thought you weren't going to tell me what to do.'

'Just don't do it for the wrong reasons. Don't finish it between us as a way of punishing yourself.'

'Punishing myself for what?' she said.

'You've felt guilty all along,' he said.

'I feel even guiltier now. This isn't what I want, but it's the way it has to be. I'm sorry, Steve. I really do have to go now.'

As she ended the call, she heard a noise from the bedroom behind her. She wondered what she would say when he asked her why she hadn't woken him up. Before turning round, she had a last look at the eastern sky. Venus could still be seen, but Saturn had completely faded away.

· THE LARDER ·

Not long after we got together, she mentioned that when she was a child her older sister had taken her treasured copy of *The Observer's Book of Birds* and destroyed it. She could still picture the two thrushes on the cover. I tried some secondhand bookshops, but could only find a later edition, so, although I knew it would be easy to find a copy online, I decided to give her my own, featuring on the dustjacket what I knew, more precisely, to be a pair of fieldfares. I had bought it secondhand a year earlier, having decided to start collecting the Observer's Books, but only those of a particular vintage, reissues from the late 50s and early 60s.

A week after I had given it to her, I found myself briefly on my own in her kitchen and happened to spot the book lying on the worktop. I picked it up and noticed that the front jacket flap had been inserted between two pages – between the garden warbler and the Dartford warbler – like a bookmark.

I heard the creak of a loose floorboad on the landing outside the kitchen and immediately put the book down again and knelt to get the milk out of the fridge. As she entered the kitchen, I saw her eyes flick to the book momentarily.

'Cup of tea?' I offered.

'Thanks.'

While the kettle was boiling, I visited the bathroom. I

heard her leave the kitchen. When I came out, I saw that the book had gone from the worktop.

As I was pouring the tea, she re-entered the kitchen and stood behind me. I turned around.

She was standing very close. I handed her one of the mugs.

'Thank you,' she said as she took a sip.

'You're welcome.'

She didn't back away.

'I like your flat,' I said.

'Good,' she said. 'I want you to feel at home.'

She took another sip of her tea and I tried my own, but it was too hot.

'Where do those doors lead?' I asked, inclining my head towards two doors off a narrow vestibule leading to the bathroom.

'The green door leads outside,' she said. 'Backyard. There are steps down. It doesn't get much use over the winter.'

'It's spring now,' I pointed out.

'Shall we go and sit in the sitting room where we can be more comfortable?' she said.

'OK,' I said and followed her, with a backwards glance at the other door, which had been stripped and coated in woodstain.

The walls of the sitting room were bare apart from a framed pastel of heathland dotted with clumps of gorse.

'I know I've asked you before,' I said. 'Is that of somewhere in particular?'

'The New Forest,' she said.

'That's where you're from, somewhere down there.'

Later, she was in the kitchen preparing a snack for us to have before we went out for a drink. She sang to herself as I listened from the bedroom. She had a lovely, rippling singing voice with just an occasional harsh, almost scolding, note to it. I saw the book by her side of the bed and picked it up. The jacket flap remained in the same place. 'This uncommon little warbler is the only resident bird of its family,' I read from the description of the Dartford warbler. 'It is found only in a few southern counties.' I scanned down the page. 'HAUNT. Gorse bushes and copses.' Then, hearing her approaching from the kitchen, I put the book back down, making sure the flap stayed in the same place.

We saw each other only once a week, as we lived in different cities. On a Monday or Tuesday, I would catch a train and we would spend the night together.

The following week, I arrived in the afternoon while she was still at work. I made a pot of tea and while it was brewing I looked idly around the kitchen, pretending to myself I wasn't looking for *The Observer's Book of Birds*. I looked at the door to the backyard; it was actually painted the greenish blue of a small number of British birds' eggs – heron, dunnock, redstart, whinchat. (I had recently acquired a fine copy of *The Observer's Book of Birds' Eggs*.) There was a key in the lock. I looked at the door next to it, which did not have a key in its lock, but then maybe it wasn't locked. I poured out the tea, then went over and grasped the handle of the woodstained door. I turned the handle. The door was locked. I moved to my right and unlocked the greenish blue door. Wooden steps led down to another door at the bottom. I went down, unlocked that door and found myself in a yard no more than six feet square. There was a little round table and two chairs. It was a fine day, warm enough to sit outside. I went back upstairs for my tea.

There wasn't much else in the yard. A washing line hung down from a hook. Its other end lay coiled on the concrete flags next to a hefty stone around which I noticed a number of smashed snails' shells. I sat and drank my tea until the sun disappeared behind a cloud and I went back inside.

When she came home we went out to the pub. I watched her as she walked to the bar for our second round. She was wearing a deceptively simple dress that flattered her. She had wide hips and narrow ankles; her bare arms tapered to slender wrists and long, elegant fingers that rested on the edge of the bar the way they might settle on a piano keyboard.

I smiled at her as she returned with our drinks.

Later, in the flat, I leaned back against the kitchen sink and she pressed into me. I threaded my arms around her waist and kissed her.

'I sat in the yard this afternoon,' I said.

'Really?' she said, returning my kiss.

'Yeah. It's nice.'

She laughed.

'What's that other door?' I asked, indicating with a nod the one I meant.

'That's the larder,' she said, pulling away from me and taking both my hands in hers. 'Shall we go to bed?'

'I can't think of a good reason not to,' I said and let her lead me out of the kitchen. I had only a very limited view from behind, but her expression looked strangely fixed and almost alien as her sharp features cut through the still air. We both in turn stepped on the loose floorboard.

In the middle of the night I woke with a pounding head. She stirred as I got up, but her breathing remained slow and steady.

I found some paracetamol in the bathroom and gulped two down with a glass of water. Sensing that I would struggle to get back to sleep, I went into the sitting room. On the coffee table was *The Observer's Book of Birds*. I picked it up. There was enough light from the streetlights, the blinds having not been lowered. The flap had been moved on by a single page to the thrushes – mistle thrush and song thrush. My eyes moved over the text until they snagged on a short paragraph towards the bottom of the page devoted to the song thrush: 'FOOD. Worms, slugs, snails, grubs and insects; also berries. The bird smashes the snail-shells on a stone known as an "anvil".'

The following week the papers were talking about a heatwave. She texted me, saying did I fancy meeting her by the canal and we could walk back up towards her neighbourhood, perhaps getting something to eat.

When I reached the canal she was already there, standing on the road bridge looking down into the water. Unaware of my approach, she appeared to be staring with almost murderous intensity at a moorhen and her chicks.

'What did they ever do to you?' I joked.

She snapped her head round and her smile of recognition took a moment to arrive. She pecked me on the lips and we headed in a north-easterly direction, ending up walking through the market. I had previously seen the lock-up shops down there only after the end of trading, all the units hidden away behind roller shutters covered in vivid graffiti. Every other business, it seemed, was an African butcher's, their trestle tables practically lowing under stacks of cows' hooves.

'Look at these,' she said, pointing to yet more hooves

hanging from lethal meat-hooks just above eye-level. She took hold of my hand for the first time during the walk, intertwining her long fingers with mine. I looked down involuntarily and was aware of her turning to look at me, so I met her gaze. There was a strange half-smile on her lips that didn't quite reach her eyes. She looked back at the meat-hooks. The butcher approached from the shadows, asking if he could help us, but she turned away without answering him and we walked on.

When we reached the main road, she asked if I was hungry and without waiting for an answer headed for the first of several Turkish restaurants that lined the high street.

She tore at a shish kebab with her teeth as I tried to keep pace, then we bought some beers from the off-licence across the road and took them back to hers, where we drank them slouched on the sofa in front of the television. Without warning, she stood up and put out her hand. I let her pull me to my feet and followed her into the bedroom, where she quickly undressed and got into bed. I looked down at her, becoming aware of *The Observer's Book of Birds* on her bedside table.

'I just need to go to the bathroom,' I said.

As I passed through the kitchen I looked at the two doors on the left. My eye was drawn to the stained door, which in the light from the window appeared a dark rusty red. For the first time since I had been coming to the flat, this door had a key in its lock. I walked on into the bathroom, where I emptied my bladder and quickly cleaned my teeth before going back through the kitchen and on to the landing, where the loose floorboard creaked beneath my feet.

As soon as I got into bed, she sat up and knelt over me, then kissed me. I felt her teeth pressing behind her lips. I kept thinking about the book that was within arm's reach, plus my stomach had started to ache, presumably from the meat-heavy meal. We soon finished and she got up to go to the bathroom while I reached over and picked up the book. The cover flap had been moved forward about ten pages. I glanced at the nightingale on the left-hand page, then turned to the red-backed shrike on the right. I read: 'This summer visitor from Africa is well named "Butcher Bird", as it butchers birds, mice and insects, and impales them on thorns and spikes, known as its "larder".' I heard the creak of the loose floorboard and quickly closed the book and put it back.

She went to sleep within minutes of getting back into bed, whereas I lay awake for what seemed like hours, unable to relax.

The pain in my gut woke me in the night. I thought at first it was serious, but as I came fully awake I realised it had not got any worse. I could hear her breathing, low and regular. I got out of bed and walked softly out of the room. I stepped around the loose floorboard and entered the kitchen. I went into the bathroom but failed to make anything happen that might have eased my stomach ache. Instead I returned to the kitchen and stared at the door to the larder. I looked at the key in the lock. The next thing I knew I was holding the rough-textured key between my finger and thumb, turning it, then twisting the door handle.

As I started opening the door I heard a noise – not the squeak of a hinge that needed oiling, but the familiar creak of the loose floorboard on the landing.

· THE GOLDFINCH ·

I'm crossing the tram tracks in the main square when I see him. He's walking away from the library; I'm heading towards it. His jacket is a little shiny but his face has seen a razor this morning. I pass in front of a tram and when I look back there's no sign of him. I search the interior of the tram in case he's got on, but can't see him. He could be at the far side of the square in the time it takes the tram to disgorge its passengers and acquire new ones.

Of course, I know it isn't Paul Martens. For a start, he would be a long, long way from home, so it would be a strange coincidence, and secondly Paul Martens died in a road accident when we were both sixteen. It's just someone who looks like him. Someone who looks exactly like Paul Martens would look if he had reached his early forties, as I have.

I'm sorry I didn't get a longer look at the man, but I'm grateful for the distraction. Any distraction, however minor, is welcome these days.

Tomorrow I start to fast. Liquid diet, for the first day, blended soups and smooth yoghurts. Then, the second day, liquid diet for real. Drinks only, no food whatsoever. I can't even boil a chicken bone. Like I might want to. Third day, laxatives. Everything turns to water and your gut is a boiler.

Day four: you try to stand up, get to hospital. Somehow. You lie down and in they go.

In they go to find out where it is and how big it is and back out they come and you read their lips for any of several key words: *sorry, inoperable, weeks, comfortable.*

Having dropped off my library books, I return to the outskirts of town. Spotting the familiar outline of the abandoned bleach works, I decide to go and see Nadine, whose place is across the street from its graffiti-decorated exterior wall. I know her headaches have come back. Nadine's worn a hat for as long as I've known her. She has a few different ones, but I've never seen her without either the brown suede cap or the blue woollen beret. Someone introduced me to Nadine when I moved here a couple of years ago. Later they told me she was terminal. Who isn't, I asked? No, really, they said. Two years, three at the most. The hats are to hide hair loss and scars. But the effect for me is to make her scars seem more terrible, because I imagine them travelling all over her scalp like railway tracks.

When I turn up, a school party is just leaving.

Every few weeks, the doctors slide Nadine through the CAT scanner to check the size of the tumour. Has it grown bigger? Has it shrunk? Sometimes, when it's grown in size, they go in and trim it back.

What they do with the dead around here – with Nadine and another friend of mine called Marc, who has more tumours than he has healthy organs – is they separate them from their partners, then keep them ticking over and organise visits for schoolchildren. Nadine and Marc could say no if they wanted to, but it's part of the culture. To refuse is bad manners. It's also pointless. You do have the option of insisting that you and your partner stay together, but it doesn't work, because in any real sense the separation has already taken place.

One of you dies, the other is left behind, at the moment of diagnosis.

So the dead go along with it and within weeks or even days the first parties are booked in. Nadine doesn't leave the house much now, so the children come to her. Marc can still get around the park, accompanied by his German shepherd and, often as not, by a crowd of schoolkids as well who watch the way he walks – slowly, with exaggerated care – and touch his papery hands. The jargon says it's to help the children become familiarised with death, not to fear it. Death is part of the process. Life is a cycle.

I could have done with some of that when I was a kid. Death was a mystery then, a secret. Code words mouthed soundlessly in the presence of children. My father was dead for a long time before he actually died. He spent his too-short life lurching from one scare to the next, half-heartedly reaching for his few scarce pleasures – whisky, hillwalking, Shostakovich – during the brief interludes when he wasn't convinced that tumours were growing inside him like bad apples on a poisoned tree.

Nadine and I sit on her couch, close enough that I could reach out a hand and touch her arm. She's wearing the brown cap. She looks tired after the school visit. On her mantelpiece is a single framed photograph of her parents. She doesn't keep any pictures of Stefan, her ex, on view because seeing them would hurt too much. She sees me looking at it. Do you want to pass it to me, she asks? She runs her fingertips over the image of her parents caught in bright, slanting autumn sunlight. My father used to take me birdwatching, she says. We were on holiday somewhere, I don't remember where, and we kept seeing goldfinches. Every time we went out we would see one. Perched on a thistle, pecking at a teasel. Flying out of the hedgerow across the road in front of the car. You'd recongise the flash of red, the little red face. Do you know, the goldfinch is pictured on the front cover of just about every bird book ever published?

I didn't know that.

It is, she says. And do you know something else? My father told me this. We were driving down one particular country lane and suddenly he stopped the car and pointed. Look, he said, through the windscreen! We were all silent as we looked, trying to see what he was talking about, and then I noticed the little red and white face and the black wings with yellow bars. And as we carried on watching, I realised there were several of them in this bush. I'd never seen more than one at a time before. It felt like, I don't know, like a blessing or something. It felt special, like we had stepped outside of the normal rules for a privileged moment. Like how you feel when you see a fox in the street. Everything goes quiet and still. And then my father's foot relaxed on the brake pedal and the car rolled forward a fraction and the movement frightened the birds and they all flew off.

And as we all breathed out, my father told us that the collective noun for goldfinches is a 'charm'. A charm of goldfinches. Isn't that beautiful?

I look at Nadine and see that her eyes are full of sharp points of light.

Apparently, she adds, in medieval times the goldfinch was believed by some to be an effective charm against the plague. Hence the collective noun, I suppose.

I hold her gaze but say nothing.

Anyway, she says, how are *you*?

I'm fine, I lie.

My father used to take me walking in the hills, I tell

her. We would walk for hours on end. Every now and then he would stop and look at the map, giving me a chance to catch up, and more or less as soon as I did he'd set off again. Sometimes we'd see birds of prey, but I didn't know if they were sparrowhawks or peregrines or merlins and my father was always too far ahead, so I categorised them according to my own distinctions. This one had wing tips that were more pointed than that one. That one hovered, this one soared. Eventually we would reach whatever summit or cairn or trig point my father had been aiming for and we would stop and eat the bread and cheese in his rucksack.

Merlins are very small, she tells me, as she hands me back the photograph of her parents. Tiny.

I remember the first time I saw an owl, I tell her. I was amazed by how small it was. You hear about owls and hawks and falcons. You hear all these fabulous stories about them and they loom large in your imagination, and then you see one and they can be surprisingly small.

I replace the photograph on the mantelpiece next to what looks like a piece of driftwood. I run my fingers over it to feel the grain, expecting the smoothness of the sea.

A friend carved that for me, Nadine says, smiling. Paolo. He works with broken bits of wood. He loves storms. He goes out collecting branches blown off trees.

Day 1

After a late breakfast of tea and fruit juice, I go rummaging in my stationery drawer. Somewhere I know I have a scalpel, its blade sunk in a chunk of cork. I used it for craft when I was younger and still had a desire to make things such as personalised cards. Over the years I have occasionally come across it in this drawer full of dried-up ballpoints and exhausted felt tips, plastic rulers, scratched protractors and propelling pencils without any lead. Seeing it would always bring back memories of the cards I made with it. I never threw it away because I always knew I might want it again one day, like everything else in that drawer. And yet now, when I do want it, I can't find it.

Bent over a piece of card with a pair of scissors, which are harder to work with and will produce a less satisfactory result, I realise where the scalpel has gone. I haven't misplaced it or forgotten where it is kept. I haven't thrown it out during a purge of unwanted clutter. It has simply fallen out of use. Unused for so long, now it has ensured it may no longer *be* used. It has simply leached out of my life. Like the old jacket of my father's that I wore every day, until it began to look shabby, and then left in a wardrobe for too long before going to look for it again, only to find it gone. And like the recording of Bartók's string quartets I listened to all the time in my twenties, which I grew tired of in my thirties and then wanted to hear again a few years ago, but couldn't find. The flimsy sleeve treated me to a hollow laugh as I pulled it from the shelf after too many years of neglect.

I supposed at the time that I had forgotten and left the jacket at the dry-cleaners some years before. And maybe I'd mistakenly left the Bartók on the turntable when throwing out the stereo having bought a new one. That these were unconvincing rationalisations never really worried me.

Day 2

There is a dull ache in my stomach. This is not the pain that first rang alarm bells, in conjunction with other symptoms, which has been with me on and off for several weeks. This is hunger. The original pain was white and round like a snowball; the hunger pangs are grey streaks. Instead of suffering the diarrhoea that had been concurrent with the white pain, I now find myself constipated.

Because of the constant hunger, which gnaws at my stomach like a rat behind a wall, I cannot distract myself from what is happening to me. I try, by finishing off the card for Nadine, but there is no escape from it. I visualise what I'm convinced is living inside me, consuming me as it metastasises.

Day 3

I do not leave the bathroom for longer than two minutes. I do not stand up straight for longer than five. I want to go out and post the card, but that's impossible. I can hardly walk, doubled over with pains both grey and white and now red, for the liquid fire pouring out of me.

Day 4

I drive the car with extreme difficulty. My throat is dry, my head throbbing. The taste of the grave is in my mouth. I have not eaten for more than three days. It is the first time in my life I have gone for so long without food. I feel simultaneously horrified and almost proud. Proud that I have shown I can treat my body with the same degree of uncompromising brutality as the disease itself. *Anything you can do…*

I stop at the traffic lights. To get to the hospital I need to turn left.

Down the road to the right, however, I see a postbox.

When the lights change I turn right and pull over. I post the card, get back into the car and drive on. The road to the hospital recedes in my rear-view mirror. I keep on driving past the next intersection and gradually the city dismantles itself around me until I am driving through the forest with wild boar and pine martens staring at me, unseen, from between the brown boles of tightly packed firs. The gradient steepens imperceptibly at first, then the road is forced to tack from side to side to continue its climb, and the trees thin out before falling away altogether and revealing a bleak vista of hills.

I leave the car where my father always used to leave his, and climb over the low wall to pick up the path and begin walking. Within five minutes I am sweating and my legs feel as if they are about to give way. I sense, however, that the effort required to keep going at this stage is largely mental. I try to dissociate my mind from my failing body. I am no longer feeling pain so much as emptiness, as if my body is a condemned building that is being stripped for demolition. If the emptiness has a colour it is black. At the same time as I decide this, I become aware of black flecks at the edges of my vision. They move erratically. Visual disturbance? An unkindness of ravens? I hear a dry ratcheting cry that reminds me more of magpies – a tidings of magpies – but I know there would be no magpies out here, and when I hear it for the second time I realise it's the sound of my own laughter.

In the language of therapy, I learned my father's behaviour, acquiring his lifelong phobia as if it were infectious. As a child I followed him along these same mountain paths; now two sets of prints have merged into one. I find this funny. I don't have any bread and cheese, but I don't need any. I have gone beyond hunger. I would rather die of starvation out here than be drip-fed my own death. I've no one to be separated from, but I don't need the school parties, the tiny inquisitive hands and big round eyes. A repeated phrase from the Bartók string quartets comes into my mind. I liked the Bartók principally because it seemed to presage the inevitable. It was laced through with unease, yet it never frightened me. I was drawn to the palindromic patterns of the fourth quartet. But my response was not so much intellectual as visceral. The high-pitched *glissandi* sounded to me like a bow being drawn across the muscle fibres of my heart.

Sometimes the things that fall out of your life come back. A favourite blue T-shirt came back, but it had a hole in it. The Bartók came back. I discovered it one day in my collection, hiding in the wrong sleeve as if it had been there all along, but something had happened to it. There was a jump in the fourth quartet. It was unplayable.

I see a figure in the distance, standing still against the horizon, the height of a man. Two skylarks spring out of the tussocky grass by my side, climbing two invisible spiral staircases in a mocking display of a double helix. They'd do better to heed the hover of a goshawk, which must have strayed from the forests of the lower slopes. I look up, trying to follow the skylarks' spiralling flight accompanied by a drunken burble of song. I see them, tiny fast-moving dots, motes in the eye. The goshawk has disappeared, but I can still hear its mewing cry like that of a buzzard. Invisible, the goshawk is lethal. It will dive in from one side for the kill.

The figure has no arms. It appears to jump around in the otherwise fixed landscape ahead of me. A hallucination? My legs keep going and within an impossibly short time I'm there next to it, touching it. The rough gritstone under my hands. The finger-width gaps between one stone and the next. A cairn. I collapse, my shoulders resting against it. My head falls backwards. Contact. My heart slows down. The sky darkens. My head falls forward. A buzzard's cry escapes from my lips.

I wake with no sense of time having passed. Vague feelings of discomfort. Figures moving around me. White shapes, faces a blur, voices booming. I try to shrug off the druggy effect and listen to what's being said. *Nothing to find.* I feel lightheaded, try to sit up, but fall back down. Woozy, as if drunk. Unsteady. *All clear.* I fall backwards. My head makes contact and everything is dark again.

A light wind wakes me, feathering my skin. Gritstone against the back of my head. I feel nothing below my stomach. That part of my body has become alien through its betrayal. My head pounding, I get to my feet and move around the cairn, looking into the distance for the next one and beginning to walk, slowly, towards it. For a few steps my father falls in line just in front of me, his own battle with the long-feared disease fought and lost, and as he turns to look at me, as if to see how far back I have fallen, I stumble, and when I look up again he has gone. But in his place, approaching me as I am drawn forward towards it, is the next cairn. I don't remember them being so close together and indeed I wonder if they are, because when I look back I can't see the previous one. Have I been walking in a circle? Is this a trap?

I allow one knee to fold and as the other is unable to hold my weight on its own I fall to the ground. I pass in and out of consciousness and scan the horizon for birds. If I could see another bird now, I would feel this was worth it. I would be glad of the decisions that have brought me here. Instead, angling sideways across the slope of the hill I see a man coming towards me. Because of the position in which I am lying I cannot get a good look at his face. Failing to stop at a respectful distance he comes right up to me and kicks out at the cairn. But it's my stomach that registers the impact of his boot.

You stupid fuck, he says to me. You stupid fucking fuck.

I curl into a ball, expecting another kick, which doesn't come.

Fuck you, I try to say, but my mouth is too dry.

Sit the fuck up, you stupid fuck.

I do so with agonising difficulty.

So you're the disease, I say?

You know who I am, you fuck.

I squint at him against the late sunlight. The shabby jacket, a bit of a shine to the material, something sticking out of the top pocket.

Paul, I say in a croaking, broken voice. Paul Martens. You died in a road accident.

No, you fuck, he shouts, getting angrier.

We were friends, I say, weakly.

Friends? *Friends?* You dropped me, you fuck.

I try to remain upright.

I didn't die. The accident was staged, he says, his voice dropping for the first time. I guess you would say I just fell out of your life.

So saying, he aims a boot at my kneecap. I don't feel anything, just hear something snap. Then I feel sick.

Every now and then you'd think of me, and then you'd forget me again, he says, leaning closer. And then you forgot me altogether.

My head spins, like when I close my eyes after a night of drinking to forget.

Everything comes back, he says, almost offhand. Those things that fall out of your life, they all come back.

My eyes remain closed most of the time now, opening only briefly.

Do you like my jacket, he asks?

Should I recognise it?

Of course. You silly, stupid fuck. And guess what I've got in the top pocket.

Like I care.

He takes the scalpel from the top pocket, then dips his free hand into one of the other pockets and brings out something small, fragile, alive. He gets down on one knee so I get a better view. He extends his left arm. In his hand he holds a tiny goldfinch, its head twisting this way and that as it tries to escape. I can see the delicate feathered skin of its white neck pulsating, can almost feel its hot little body in my own hand, wriggling, desperate to fly.

He takes the scalpel and draws it in a circle around the head of the bird. There is an almost inaudible crack, and the head is free. The little red, white and black head. He reaches up and places it on the top of the cairn.

I feel myself becoming lighter as wind rushes past me and a lurching sensation in my stomach suggests upward movement. I look back down and see a single body slumped by the cairn. As I look up again, I am aware of a blur of black and yellow. Then blue. Nothing but blue.

· THE KESTREL AND THE HAWK ·

I reach the island by train. As I start walking from the station into the village, I immediately hear a noise behind me that can only be a jet aircraft approaching at speed. I look up; the sky is clear and blue. I turn to see a black shape cross in front of the sun and a second later the jet is over my head, the volume of noise and a sense of compression in the air combining to exhilarating effect. I start counting as the Hawk passes directly overhead, then descends a further fifty feet over the fields and makes its final approach to runway 32 at RAF Valley.

A second Hawk passes overhead exactly twenty seconds after the first one.

There will be a gap of five minutes or so until the next pair.

Rhosneigr manifests itself initially as a series of sprawling caravan sites and pebble-dash bungalows, then larger houses, rental properties, guest villas. It's a village of second homes, a ghost town out of season, but this is July and middle-class families from Manchester and the West Midlands are installed outside the cafés on and off Station Road eating French pastries and drinking cappuccino and freshly squeezed orange juice.

A waitress appears. She's in her late twenties with ash-blonde hair held in a bun by a distinctive yellow-and-black Staedtler pencil, a few loose strands falling across her face and needing to be tucked behind her ear from time to time. She has good cheekbones and a scattering of faint freckles. Her eyes are the grey of paving stones or pebble-dash. She looks as if she could have done with another hour in bed, but I imagine she always looks like this. She nods at the bag I have looped over the back of my chair and says, 'You here for the birds?'

I nod and smile.

'I was watching a kestrel over the dunes the other morning,' she says, 'before coming here.' She gestures absently around the café terrace and then looks down the street and stands in profile to me with her mouth slightly open as if suddenly transported back to the dunes. The momentary quiet is shattered by the approach of another jet. The waitress's eyes flick up as a small black aircraft appears in the sky and passes out of view, like a fly on a television screen. The loose strands of hair fall across her cheek as she turns back to face me and asks what I would like.

I take my time over a strong black coffee and a plate of eggs. A woman at the neighbouring table excitedly tells her grown-up daughter that Prince William is at the air base. The daughter is distracted by her own small child and says, 'Hmm?'

'Prince William,' says the older woman.

'What's he doing?' asks the daughter. 'Inspecting the troops?'

'No, silly. He's learning to fly. Getting his wings. That might have been him just now going over, you never know.'

'You never know,' the daughter repeats, wiping up spilled baby food from the table.

I leave a tip – generous, but not too generous – and walk down the street to the beach, my bag over my shoulder. As I reach the beach, two more Hawks come in to land, separated again by twenty seconds. I look at my watch to find out the exact time. The base is a quarter of a mile to my right, hidden from the beach by a line of dunes. I head down to where the sand is firmer and then turn right, walking parallel with the high-tide line. I walk neither too fast nor too slowly. The waitress's face enters my mind. The splash of freckles across her nose. Her tired grey eyes – heron grey, gull-wing grey. Even the unconscious swing of her hip as she turned to go and place my order. At the far end of the beach, a house sits on a promontory. A white house, isolated, windows staring out to sea, a house Edward Hopper might have painted. I switch my bag from my right shoulder to my left and walk on.

To reach the dunes I have to cross a narrow channel. I remove my boots and socks and roll up my trousers. The water reaches to just below the knee. A shoal of tiny fish is disturbed by my crossing. On the other side I walk up into the dunes barefoot, avoiding the thistles that sprout among the marram grass and sea spurge. When I reach the top of the dunes I get my first look at RAF Valley less than a hundred yards away. I sit down and put my socks and boots back on. Two glossy black Hawks are taxiing into position for take-off. I slip the bag from my shoulder and undo the drawstring. I pull out a bulky cushioned case and release its clasp. From inside I take a telescopic sight, then close the case. I rest my elbows on my knees and train the sight on the first of the two jets.

The Hawk is a tandem-cockpit aircraft. The student sits in the front, his QFI in the rear cockpit. These stubby, low-wing machines, their Rolls-Royce engines capable of 6500 pounds of thrust and speeds of over 550 knots, are used in the RAF only as advanced trainers and by the Red Arrows. I focus on the student pilot of the first plane, the lower half of his face clearly visible. Out of a thoroughness that's akin to superstition, I examine the pilot of the second plane, too.

Once the Hawks have taken off, a Land Rover parked at the south-eastern end of the runway rolls on to the tarmac and I hear a cacophony of raucous and aggressive bird calls. Two crows that had been perched on a wooden fence just beyond the edge of the airfield lift lazily into the air and settle on the grass no more than a few feet away. The bird calls continue, but the crows are happy where they are. After a minute or so of bird calls, the Land Rover pulls off the runway and parks up on the grass between the runway and the taxiway. The bird calls have ceased. I check my watch, then open the case.

Another Hawk approaches from the south-east. I see the light, hear the sound. I lie down on my stomach and put my eye to the telescopic sight. As the pilot clears the perimeter fence I can see the set of his jaw. I switch to the second plane and follow it in from distance, my hand free of any tremor. I edge around, watching the second plane touch down, hearing the squeal of rubber on tarmac.

Prince William is not at RAF Valley to fly Hawks. Flight Lieutenant Wales was awarded his wings two years ago. He is here to undertake Search and Rescue pilot training in Sea King 3As. Even as I swivel around to scope out the yellow helicopters parked close to the airport buildings I spot a group of four men in full flying gear making their way towards these aircraft. The tallest of them walks second from the left. I loosen my shoulders, uncurl my fingers, set myself.

Out of the corner of my eye I see a shape in the sky

above the dunes. I look up. A kestrel is hovering, its tail fanned, wings beating fast, head still as a rock. I see the waitress's face, her eyes, slate grey, gunmetal grey, and when I look back at the airfield, the four men have gone.

· THE LURE ·

As a young man I lived in Paris for a year, in the northeastern corner of the city, the 19th *arrondissement*. My nearest métro station was Bolivar but I almost never used it. Jaurès may have been further away, but it was a pleasant walk down Avenue Secrétan, past the *boulangerie*, the *épicerie*, the *charcuterie*. Past the cheap supermarket – Monoprix or Franprix. I can't remember. It was a long time ago.

I was teaching English in a school on Rue de Seine in the 6th, so I used to take line 5, *direction* Place d'Italie, from Jaurès to Gare du Nord and then change to line 4, *direction* Porte d'Orléans. I would get off at Odéon, then walk up Boulevard Saint-Germain and turn right up Rue de Seine. I used to enjoy the various colours of the different times of day. In the morning everything seemed golden, the polished brass and gilt of the shop fronts, the windows full of *pains* and *baguettes*, the early autumn sun flashing on the flanks of passing trains on the elevated métro line at Jaurès – line 2. By late afternoon, when I left the school to walk back down Rue de Seine, everything had turned red. Giant hams and sausages, the scarlet faces of pheasants hanging by their feet. Beaujolais sloshing into glasses at pavement cafés. As I descended into the métro at Odéon, the sun would be suspended in the sky behind me like half a blood orange. By the time I emerged from underground at Jaurès, the sun would have set.

I first saw him on the final leg of my homeward journey one Friday afternoon in October. He sat with his guide dog at his feet. He wore glasses – an old, unfashionable frame with smeary, fingerprinted lenses. There was something about his eyes. They weren't right, somehow. He was sitting diagonally across from me, on the other side of the aisle, so my view was not the best, but I couldn't tear my eyes from him. He alighted, as I did, at Jaurès, but while I made for the exit, he veered off to change to line 7b, *direction* Pré-Saint-Gervais.

He was of average height and appeared to be in his late fifties, the same age as my father. Iron-grey hair, stiff as wire wool. A crumpled, resigned look to his jowly features. But the eyes…

I poured myself a glass of wine before dinner and sat at the round table in the centre of my tiny studio apartment. The brown wallpaper featured large pale-coloured flowers with dark centres that thrived in the damp conditions. Yellowish artificial light filtered through the lace curtains covering the tall windows giving on to the courtyard. In the kitchen, I kept the radio permanently tuned to a jazz station. I could barely hear it, but it was the only place where I managed to get any reception at all. The shower room was located just off the kitchen and late at night I would run the hose until the shower tray was full and then sit in it listening to the radio. I missed being able to have a bath.

My single bed was pushed into a corner. There was a nightstand with a bedside light that I kept switched on at all times to try to create a little cosiness. In addition, I had Blu-tacked some postcards to the wall to give me something to look at other than the sickly flowers. On the wall facing my bed I had put up a couple of large film posters. At the foot of the bed was a door that the landlord had advised me would remain locked. It was partly glazed, like an interior door, but both the glass and the wooden panel below it were papered over with the same extravagant blooms.

I lifted my wine glass to my lips and thought about the man on the métro. It was not uncommon to see blind people wearing glasses, of course. He could be partially sighted. But the odd thing, I realised as I got a *demi-baguette* from the kitchen and took a knife to the Boursin, was his fixed stare. I couldn't remember seeing him blink.

I saw him again a couple of weeks later. It was a Sunday and I had gone to have lunch at the apartment of a colleague, an older woman whom I knew only as Madame Villemain. On my originally taking up my duties at the school at the beginning of the autumn term, my fellow English teachers, all of them French, had not been overly friendly. I had put this down to what I regarded as excessive French formality.

Madame Villemain was one of the older English teachers, in her early fifties like my mother. She commanded a certain fearful respect from the rest of the staff, smiling rarely, but she had favoured me with a flash of slightly gappy teeth on several occasions. I would smile back, taking pleasure in the illusion of complicity.

She stopped me in the corridor and asked how I was getting on. She didn't condescend to me by speaking in English. Instead, she stood very close and held my gaze with her ice-blue eyes. I was peripherally aware of a strip of lacy white undergarment visible at the open neck of her blouse. The combined aroma of coffee and cigarettes mingled with her strong body scent to produce a powerful cocktail. I felt myself start to blush and automatically lifted a hand to the side of my face. She smiled at me then but continued to speak in a low, fast voice. I was close to fluent and my understanding was better than my spoken French, but I had difficulty following her. Was she inviting me to lunch? Just me or would other people be present? Obviously I couldn't ask. She scribbled her address and phone number on a scrap of paper torn from a student's homework and handed it to me before turning to go. Suddenly I was alone in the corridor, unsure what had just taken place, my face burning. I felt, somehow, as if her eyes were still on me.

Madame Villemain's home was a large apartment in an ancient building on the Île Saint-Louis. Out of breath from my climb to the fourth floor, I was taken aback when the door to the apartment was opened by a tall, gaunt man with a wide forehead and shoulder-length black hair streaked with grey. He failed to introduce himself beyond shaking my hand and issuing a grunt. He retreated into a book-lined study while Madame Villemain ushered me out on to a little balcony. While I stared at the view over the river, Madame Villemain's blue eyes seemed to bore into the side of my head. I asked about Monsieur Villemain and briefly turned to look at her, to catch a flare of irritation in her eye. She used her hands to make a dismissive gesture and muttered something about Freud, Jacques Lacan and the Université de Paris.

Over a lunch of salad and cold meats, she watched me while her husband pushed his plate to one side and lit a cigarette. He had been talking about his work; his wife's apparent lack of interest must have been as obvious to him as it was to me, but he seemed indifferent in turn. When he had finished his cigarette, he pushed back his chair and left the room. Madame Villemain and I then discussed the Luc Besson film, *Subway*, which we had both seen, separately, the week before. I confessed to having most enjoyed the look of the film, its fluorescent glimmer, while Madame Villemain gave a dark smile and made a remark about the film's star, Christophe Lambert. She used an idiomatic expression that was unknown to me, but its general tenor was clear and I looked down at my empty plate, embarrassed. She immediately apologised and placed her hand on my arm. I transferred my gaze from my plate to her hand: tanned from a summer spent in the Midi, it was marked by spots of sun damage that revealed her age. I imagined her long, tapering fingers pressing into the flesh of my bare back.

Monsieur Villemain could be heard opening the door of his study. I looked at Madame Villemain, waiting for her to release my arm before her husband entered the room. She did so only at the last moment, but continued to hold my gaze while Monsieur Villemain rooted about for something in a bureau at the far side of the room. I expected him to sense the tension in the air, but he paid neither of us the slightest heed. I left shortly afterwards, when Madame Villemain said she wanted to have a lie-down. I half-imagined that it was intended as an invitation, even with her husband in the apartment.

I crossed the river via the Pont Marie and instead of descending into the métro continued walking. If you had asked me, I would have said I was wandering at random, but as Dr Freud understood, a man walking in a city is controlled by forces he may not even be aware of. I soon found myself walking up Rue Saint-Denis. At the lower end of the street, the young, lithe girls in their 20s and 30s in their bustiers and suspenders were of no interest to me. Regulation erotica for sexual conformists. Each to his own. It wasn't until I had crossed Rue Réaumur that my responses began to remind me of Madame Villemain's apartment on the Île Saint-Louis – without the tension provided by the presence of Monsieur Villemain, perhaps, but then the absence of touch began to create another, very particular tension.

I looked at each woman in every doorway and as my gaze slithered over exposed flesh and plunged into areas of shadow, I felt as if my eyes were an extension of my sense of touch. As on previous visits to this part of town, it was on Rue Blondel that I came closest to surrendering control and crossing a threshhold I had never crossed.

On the north side of Rue Blondel, a tall, well-built woman in black stood in an open doorway at the top of a short series of steps. Statuesque, she towered over me. As I walked past, I tried to make sense of what she was wearing. It revealed a certain amount and yet still contrived to leave much to the imagination. Mostly she seemed to be covered by a filmy veil, or veils, a fine mesh, offering a partial view of a magnificent décolletage and long, strong, powerful legs. When I reached Boulevard de Sébastopol, I crossed over and walked back along Rue Blondel on the other side. After a third pass, I felt a familiar combination of intense desire and self-loathing. I hurried towards the métro at Strasbourg – Saint-Denis, but on reaching the top of the steps realised it would make more sense to keep walking up Boulevard de Strasbourg to the Gare de l'Est, which would obviate the need to change lines.

I saw him as soon as I entered the overcrowded carriage. The guide dog, the old-fashioned glasses. I was going to take a seat opposite him, but yielded to a determined-looking middle-aged woman. She said nothing, didn't even glance at me.

'*Je vous en prie, Madame,*' I said with heavy sarcasm, standing with my legs apart in the middle of the carriage.

The woman dismissed me with a glare.

The guide dog lifted its head and sniffed the air. The *signal sonore* announcing the closure of the doors rang out and the dog allowed its head to sink back down to the floor. The man's eyes did not blink and now that I was closer to him I could see why. He was wearing a mask – a rubber eye mask similar to a sleep mask but with eyes painted on to it. I couldn't tell if they were hand-painted or if the mask had been imprinted by a machine. Now I understood why he wore the glasses – to obscure the outline of the mask and soften the intensity of the painted stare – though of course now that I had seen that he was wearing a mask, the presence of the glasses seemed even more bizarre.

Closer to, he looked a little older than I had first thought – early sixties perhaps – though it was hard to be sure without seeing his eyes.

The train pulled into the platform at Gare du Nord, the *signal sonore* was heard and the doors sprang open. The blind man leaned forward and patted his dog. A large number of people got off, the woman among them, and I took her place. An Arab sat down next to the blind man, who checked on his dog again, making sure it was lying down between his feet and not blocking the way. The train was very soon back in the darkness of the tunnel. By the interior lights of the carriage I could make out the round edge of the mask at the side of the blind man's face. In fact, the mask had a slight curl on it, just above the elastic that secured it to his head, leaving a narrow black gap between rubber and skin. It wouldn't matter how long he stood in front of a mirror with his painted-on eyes, he wouldn't see that, and it would be hard to detect by touch.

The Arab got off at Stalingrad. There were now no other passengers in our immediate vicinity. I wondered if the blind man knew that someone was sitting opposite him. I imagined so. I raised my arm and waved it in the air between us. The dog stirred and the man patted the dog, murmuring reassurance. He sat back in his seat. I wanted to know what lay behind the mask. Did he have eyes at all? Were they open or closed? (Closed, surely.) What did they look like? Did they look anything like the ones painted on the mask? Had they ever worked or had he been born blind? Was it preferable to have been born blind and therefore never known what he was missing? Or to have lost his sight and therefore understand what it meant to see and have memories to draw on? Would that be a source of comfort or anguish?

At Jaurès, he got up, the dog preceding him as he headed towards the doors. I followed. When he went to change to line 7b, I still followed. I stood ten yards away on the platform. I watched him while we waited. After a couple of minutes, he turned his face towards the stillness and silence of the tunnel, and seconds later I heard the first rumblings of the approaching train. There was no doubt in my mind that he had sensed it before I did, whether he'd heard it or felt the slightest draught on his face. We were alone on the platform, and when the train arrived, the nearest carriage was empty. I followed him through the doors and remained standing while he went to sit down, led by the dog.

To my surprise he got to his feet as the train entered the next station – Bolivar. I maintained a careful distance between us as we ascended to street level. He crossed the road and walked a little way up Avenue Secrétan before turning left into a doorway between a café and a *pâtisserie*. While he was inserting his key into the lock, I drew level. I stood on the pavement and watched as he opened the door. The dog was leading him into the hallway, but he stopped and looked back. His protuberant painted eyes found mine among the passing crowds and watched me for a moment before he turned back and followed his dog into the hallway. As the door started to close, I saw his hand reach up to open his *boîte à lettres*.

Madame Villemain invited me to go with her to the Bois de Vincennes. Again, it wasn't clear to me who would be going. Part of me hoped it would be just me and Madame Villemain, and part of me didn't. She proposed that we meet at Bastille, which meant I could get line 5 from Jaurès, *direction* Place d'Italie, and stay on it past Gare du Nord and Gare de l'Est. I felt jumpy on the métro and I wasn't sure if it was due to the prospect of spending the day with Madame Villemain or the fact that I now half-expected to see the blind man whenever I descended below street level.

At Bastille I made my way to line 8, *direction* Créteil-Préfecture.

I spotted her as soon as I stepped on to the platform. She was wearing a long green woollen overcoat and had tied a gold silk scarf around her neck. I approached tentatively, but as soon as she saw me, she caught hold of my arms and offered me first one cheek and then the other. She started talking excitedly – in French – about what we were going to see or do at the Bois de Vincennes, but I was lacking key bits of vocabulary and I was distracted by her hand on my arm.

Her left hand had remained attached to my right forearm, her long ringless fingers curled around it. To emphasise certain points, she would squeeze my arm lightly. I wasn't sure if even she was aware she was doing it. There was a naturalness about it that I found exciting.

The métro arrived and its metallic doors rumbled open. It was busy and we stood leaning against the back of one of the blue-upholstered seats. Our hands touched on the vertical steel pole and neither of us hurried to reposition our fingers or apologise for the touch.

'*J'aime beaucoup le métro,*' she said. '*C'est comme si on était descendu à un autre niveau de la réalité.*'

'I don't know about another level of reality,' I said, 'but I sometimes think of it as representing our subconscious.'

'*Exactement!*'

We got off at Liberté and crossed into the park. Madame Villemain was walking quickly and I almost had to break into a trot to keep up. It was entirely possible that I was imagining something that was not happening. Madame Villemain was nothing more than a friendly colleague who had gone out of her way to make me feel a little less isolated and lonely. The fact that she and her husband appeared rather tired of each other was not unusual and it certainly didn't mean she was about to have an affair with a callow Englishman young enough to be her son.

A horseshoe-shaped crowd had gathered between the velodrome and the lake. At its centre a man in old-fashioned dress wearing a sturdy gauntlet on his left hand used his right hand to twirl a lure on the end of a long line. Suddenly, the crowd gasped and people ducked as a large bird appeared, arrowing in low and catching the baited lure in mid-air. Madame Villemain clapped her hands together in excitement and then pointed at the bird, some kind of falcon or hawk, as it settled on the grass several metres away. It held down the lure with one claw and tugged at its meaty cargo – the reward – with its large, fearsome-looking beak.

'It is an 'arris 'awk,' she told me, in English.

The falconer whistled and the bird, still clutching its prize, flew the short distance to his glove, settled and folded its magnificent wings. Deftly, like a magician, the falconer removed the lure from the hawk's grip while allowing it to keep the reward.

'Named,' Madame Villemain went on, leaning towards me conspiratorially, 'by Audubon after his great friend Edward 'arris.'

I wanted to tell Madame Villemain that I liked the way she dropped her aitches. I looked at the hawk's yellow feet gripping the falconer's gauntlet. I could feel Madame Villemain's fingers on my arm again. The hawk adopted an upright posture on the glove. The slight overhang of its brow gave it a stern expression; its eyes were the same chestnut shade as the leading edges of its wings, while the body was a darker, muddier brown. Now that it had consumed the meat, the bird was constantly switching its gaze between the falconer and the crowd, reacting to the slightest movement. Its flexible neck allowed it to turn its head almost all the way around while its body remained still.

'Look,' said Madame Villemain.

The falconer had produced a little leather hood, which he now slipped on to the bird's head from behind. The hawk accepted the imposition of the hood without protest and instantly became still.

'*La nuit est tombée*,' said Madame Villemain in my ear,

adding in English, 'It thinks it is night-time. It immediately becomes compliant.'

I turned to look at her but she was watching the hawk. A smile crept on to her lips.

At the end of the display – it continued with an eagle owl and a peregrine falcon, but it was the Harris hawk that had impressed me most deeply with its docile acceptance of temporary blindness – Madame Villemain smoked a cigarette while we walked back to the métro. Our train rattled through the tunnels and I watched the tendons in Madame Villemain's neck as she followed the toing and froing of other passengers. At one point she looked at me and I raised my eyes, too slowly. I lifted my hand to the side of my face and Madame Villemain's own hand went to the scarf at her neck, but instead of tightening it, she loosened the knot.

'I am 'ungry,' she said. 'Where do you like to eat? Take me where you like.'

I decided to take her to Chartier – or to Le Drouot. That was the problem. I knew they were two restaurants under the same ownership, but in my mind they had become one. I had eaten in both a number of times, but I didn't know which was which or how to get to either. Instead of owning up to this, I allowed Madame Villemain to think I was confident and in charge. As a result, we got off the métro at least two stops early at Strasbourg – Saint-Denis and before I knew where we were we were walking south down Boulevard de Sébastopol. We had already passed one turning on the right, which meant that Rue Blondel would be next. I knew I had made a mistake and that we needed to head west, whichever of the two restaurants was our goal, since they were located close to each other either side of Boulevard Montmartre. I couldn't suggest that we turn back, and to go straight on would only lead us further from our destination.

We turned into Rue Blondel.

'Are we going the right way?' Madame Villemain asked me.

'Yes,' I said without looking at her.

Women stood in doorways up and down the street. Many of them were about the age of Madame Villemain. I looked, because not looking seemed too obvious somehow. I never liked to do what was expected of me. I felt my skin prickling inside my clothing. I looked across the street. The tall woman in black was in her usual spot. She looked down at me and I looked away. Madame Villemain walked closer to me. I felt her arm bump softly against mine.

'It's OK,' she said, but I couldn't look at her.

We turned right at the end of the street and moments later we were walking west along Boulevard de Bonne Nouvelle.

'I think I took us the wrong way,' I said.

'It doesn't matter,' she said as she linked her arm through mine.

When we were finally sitting at a table in Le Drouot, I realised I had probably made a mistake in the choice of restaurant also. The reason I liked the place – and its sister restaurant – was because the prices were cheap and I enjoyed the legendary rudeness of the waiters. Bad wine didn't matter to me. I always drank Beaujolais and didn't know any better. But Madame Villemain would be accustomed to a better class of restaurant. To combat my nervousness, I drank quickly, and Madame Villemain matched my pace. Soon it didn't matter that the wine was a bit rough and the veal rather thin. It wasn't really about the food and drink.

We talked about school and Madame Villemain was indiscreet about colleagues. She propped her head in her hand, elbow on the table. Her shoes had been slipped off and her legs were crossed, one stockinged foot sticking out into the aisle, reminding me of my mother, who would take off her shoes in restaurants, on the few occasions we ate out, and always wore nylons. If Madame Villemain didn't retrieve it quickly enough, the waiter would catch the stray foot as he strode by. I felt certain that if I were to suggest we leave and take the métro to Jaurès, Madame Villemain would agree, but the very thought brought into my head an unwelcome image of the blind man sitting in the middle of an otherwise empty carriage, his dog at his feet.

I heard myself asking about Monsieur Villemain.

'What does he do in that study of his?' I asked. 'What's he into?'

By now we were speaking a mixture of French and English.

'Freud, mainly. The Oedipus complex,' she said, lighting a cigarette. 'Also Lacan. His theory of the Gaze. Laura Mulvey and the Male Gaze.'

'It means nothing to me,' I said, laughing.

She asked me why I had laughed and I explained that if I had said that line back home, among friends, one of them would have responded, 'Oh Vienna.'

She didn't get it. It meant nothing to her.

'You mean because of Freud?' she asked, smiling and frowning simultaneously.

'No,' I said, laughing again and dropping my hand on to hers for the first time. 'It's a line from a song.'

'So,' she said, 'are you going to take me 'ome?'

I looked at her, aware that my mouth was hanging slightly open.

'Or I can just get the métro myself,' she added.

The penny dropped. '*Non, non. Je vous accompagne.*'

Outside it was just beginning to get dark. We went down into the métro at Rue Montmartre, then changed at Strasbourg – Saint-Denis, *direction* Porte d'Orléans. We didn't talk much, just rocked with the motion of the train and watched other passengers. I asked her if she wanted to change at Châtelet, but she shook her head.

'I'll walk from the Île de la Cité,' she said.

The Seine at dusk, Notre Dame floodlit by passing Bateaux Mouches – I had heard it said that if Rome was the City of Love, Paris was the City of Lovers. As we crossed the Pont Saint-Louis I had to fight an urge to blurt out some romantic foolishness. I shoved my hands in my pockets so that they couldn't grab Madame Villemain and press her up against the stone embankment. We stopped outside her building. She removed her shoes and held them in one hand, then offered her cheek and was gone, the heavy door clicking shut after her.

At Pont Marie I skipped down the steps into the métro. I watched the other passengers through an alcoholic haze. For some reason, I wasn't at all surprised when I changed to line 5 at Gare de l'Est and found myself in the same almost empty carriage as the blind man.

I was surprised, however, when he opened his mouth and spoke: 'How are you this evening?' he said, across the space between us, in heavily accented English.

I felt as if the métro tunnel had become a lift shaft. 'What?' I stared at his unblinking eyes, which were pointed

straight at me. I moved closer to him, took a seat opposite.
'You can see,' I said, shaking my head in disbelief.

He didn't bother to answer that.

I stared at him but his face gave nothing away.

'Why did you speak to me in English?' I asked.

'Because you are English.'

The whites of his painted eyes glimmered. I looked at him, but felt as if I was seeing someone else. I tried to think of another context in which a man might speak to me from behind a mask. There was nothing sinister about the surgical mask a doctor or dentist might wear out of courtesy for you, for your benefit. You could see the eyes and the movement of the jaw, maybe even the push and pull of the fabric of the mask as words were spoken. This, though, was like speaking to an automaton or doll, although the lips moved with a naturalness that was denied by the mask. It was bewildering, alienating.

'How did you even know I was here? On this train, in this carriage?'

'I can smell you. I can smell your fear.'

I got up and looked down at him, feeling nauseous, full of violence and chaos. The dog immediately rose to its feet, a low growl building in its throat. The man reached out a hand and the dog sat back down again, but kept a wary eye on me.

'How did you know I was English?' I asked, jaw clenched.

'You spoke. You let a woman have your seat and she didn't thank you and you said, "*Je vous en prie.*" A Frenchman would never say that. A Frenchman would not be so sarcastic. Ironic, yes, perhaps, but not sarcastic. Your sarcasm was very English. Actually,' he went on, 'your accent is quite good. It was your mentality that gave you away.'

I moved across and stood by the doors.

'This is not your stop,' he said.

I needed some air. I needed to be above ground.

The doors opened and I stepped off the train. In the brief silence before the *signal sonore* I heard him mutter, ironically, '*Bonsoir, Monsieur.*'

Over the next ten days, I spent more time in my apartment than I had during recent weeks. Some evenings I got through two bottles of Beaujolais instead of my customary one. I had a lot of 'baths', listened to a fair amount of jazz.

I didn't see much of Madame Villemain. If our paths crossed, it always seemed that one of us was in a rush to do something or be somewhere. She smiled at me and I stored those smiles up. I walked the length of Rue Blondel a couple of times but I didn't climb any steps or cross any threshholds. For a few days I used different routes to get to work. I walked down Rue de Meaux to Colonel Fabien and took line 2 to Nation, then changed. Or I wandered over to Louis Blanc and took a roundabout journey on line 7, *direction* Mairie d'Ivry, getting out at Châtelet and crossing the river on foot to reach Rue de Seine. The unpredictability of these routes meant that either I was late for work, or I sat on the métro worrying that I would be late for work. And if I knew I had plenty of time I experienced non-specific anxiety instead, only it wasn't really all that non-specific.

Gingerly, I returned to line 5, changing at Gare du Nord. I did see him in the distance on one occasion, but he was at the other end of the carriage and there were enough people between us that I doubted even his sense of smell was acute enough to alert him to my presence.

I had just reached the end of a seemingly endless lesson with a class of 14-year-olds, none of whom had any interest in learning English, when I noticed Madame Villemain coming towards me in the corridor.

'Are you finished?' she asked.

So many of her questions or statements could be interpreted in a number of ways, it seemed to me. I said that I was and she demanded that I take her for a drink. We went up the road to La Palette, a few doors down from La Galerie 55, the so-called English theatre of Paris.

'Have you seen that?' she asked me, pointing with an unlit cigarette to the poster in the window advertising the theatre's latest production, *The Pink Thunderbird*.

I shook my head.

'*C'est nul*,' she said.

'I'll cross it off my list,' I said.

I remarked that she seemed agitated. She told me that Monsieur Villemain – she used his Christian name, Bernard, for the first time in my presence – was spending the evening with one of his students. The French for this – '*une de ses étudiantes*' – included more information than the same line in English would have done. Madame Villemain was jealous, but I didn't mind being used.

'*Je veux aller au cinéma*,' she said.

'*Qu'est-ce que tu veux voir?*'

'Orange mécanique.'

'*Ça se joue où?*'

Madame Villemain abandoned her cigarette in the ashtray and took that week's *Pariscope* from her bag, turning to the cinema pages. *A Clockwork Orange* was playing at Studio Galande, a short walk down Boulevard Saint-Germain. There was a screening in three-quarters of an hour. Madame Villemain said she would prefer to walk by the river.

I paid and we left, walking up Rue Guénégaud to the *quai* and turning right. She asked me if I had seen the film and I said I had been to see it in my first week in Paris. I explained about its having been withdrawn from public exhibition in England and assured her that I was more than willing to see it again. She had seen it many times, she said. It was her favourite film.

During the rape scene, she took hold of my hand.

As we left the cinema, she said she did not want to go home. In fact, what she actually said – '*Je ne veux pas rentrer chez moi*' – arguably contained a double meaning.

Emboldened by the spirit of Malcolm McDowell's portrayal of Alex DeLarge, I said, '*Vous préférez rentrer chez moi?*'

She nodded, linked my arm and we walked toward the métro at Saint-Michel. Between Etienne Marcel and Réaumur-Sébastopol, she kissed me. We changed at Gare de l'Est and on the platform for line 5, *direction* Église de Pantin, I kissed her back. I kept my eyes closed, partly because that was the normal thing to do and partly because I was afraid of whom I might see further down the platform if I opened them. We walked up Avenue Secrétan arm in arm. I apologised for my apartment because I felt I had to.

'*Vous êtes jeune*,' she said once we were inside, as if this explained – or excused – the lamentable standard of my accommodation.

I went to switch off the bedside light, but Madame Villemain requested that I leave it on.

Her hands were soft.

Afterwards, we lay together in silence. Suddenly self-conscious, I picked up my crumpled shirt from the floor and put it on, fastening a couple of buttons.

Madame Villemain lit a cigarette and looked around for an ashtray. I went and got her a side plate from the kitchen. She smoked for a few moments, then asked me to make her a coffee. I said I only had wine and she said that would do. I fetched the bottle and filled two glasses. A claw-like hand shot out to grasp one of them and she swallowed half of its contents in one go. She pointed to the half-glazed door at the foot of the bed.

'What is beyond the door?' she asked.

'Nothing. I mean I don't know. It's locked. It's got wallpaper on it.'

'I can see that. You should decorate.'

'I'm not allowed to. The landlord was very clear. The apartment stays as it is.'

'Did the school find it for you?' she asked.

I nodded.

'I have to go,' she said.

'I'll take you back,' I said.

'There is no need.'

I protested, but she insisted. She would get a taxi.

I watched her get dressed.

'This will probably not 'appen again,' she said. 'My zip, please.'

Overcome by a terrible weariness, I struggled to an upright position and helped her with her zip.

After Madame Villemain had gone, I lay awake for a long time staring at the half-glazed door at the foot of the bed. Thoughts of the falconer and his Harris hawk became jumbled up with images of Monsieur and Madame Villemain in their apartment, and of Madame Villemain in my apartment, indeed, in my bed. I slept badly, dreaming that strange noises were keeping me awake. In the morning the apartment smelt of cigarette smoke.

I stopped using the métro. I found I could no longer take the stairs down without expecting to bump into the blind man. I felt his painted eyes on me as I walked along the platform. Every time the *signal sonore* rang out and the doors snapped open, I expected to see his dog leading him into the carriage.

I discovered that I could get at least halfway to the river by walking along the Canal Saint-Martin and then there were a hundred different routes to the Left Bank that didn't go anywhere near Rue Blondel.

At school, Madame Villemain still smiled at me, but it was a kindly, motherly smile, now, more than anything. I wondered if perhaps it always had been, if what had happened had been some kind of accident, a mistake. I didn't feel any pressing need to question her about it.

Then one night I went to the kitchen to open a second bottle of wine and happened to notice, just in time, the two empty bottles on the worktop. I put the corkscrew back in the drawer and pushed the third, unopened bottle away. I walked into the shower room and leaned my hands on the sink. I had avoided mirrors for a few days after reading up on Lacan and the Gaze. I looked exactly like someone who had got through two bottles of wine in three hours. Behind me the radio played Thelonious Monk.

I left the shower room, passed through the kitchen and re-entered the bed-sitting room. I sat on the edge of the bed, thinking. I looked at the walls, at the flowers on the wallpaper, pale petals and dark centres. I looked at my film posters. I looked at the half-glazed door with its own plastering of wallpaper. I looked at the bed itself and remembered Madame Villemain lying there.

I sighed deeply and got to my feet. Putting a jacket on, I left the apartment. I turned left into the street and then left again into Rue Baste, and left once more into Avenue Secrétan. When I reached the doorway between the café and the *pâtisserie*, I had to wait ten or fifteen minutes before someone eventually exited the building. I let them get a few metres away before grabbing the door and slipping inside. I looked at the bank of *boîtes aux lettres* mounted on the wall. I had not forgotten which one was his. The second one from the left on the bottom row. Number seven, I saw. There was a name written on a piece of card in that strangely illegible handwriting that all French people seemed to have, but I wasn't particularly curious.

I passed apartments 1, 2 and 3. A door to the courtyard stood ajar. On the far side were numbers 4 and 5. I heard music coming from one of them. Another door led to a dark passageway. I pressed the timer switch, but the bulb was not working. I allowed my eyes to become accustomed to the dark, then proceeded. There was a door on the right – number 6 – and a short way after that I found number 7 on the left.

I stood in front of the door for a moment listening, but no sound came from within. I knocked once. Twice. There was no answer. All I could hear was the faint music I'd heard in the courtyard. I knocked again. Once I had decided there was no one in, I barged the door with my shoulder. With a splintering of wood, a narrow gap appeared. I gave the door another shove and it yielded. I entered and pushed the door to behind me, waiting to see if anyone would come to see what all the noise was about. No one did.

The apartment was a similar size to mine, but the layout was different. I had entered directly into the kitchen. There were some dirty pots and cutlery both in the sink and on the work surface. They had not been left to soak: the food on them was congealed and would be difficult to remove. There was a head of garlic on top of the fridge. It was dried out, little more than a husk. Some overripe tomatoes sat in a chipped bowl on a shelf. At the left-hand end of the kitchen, behind a plastic curtain, was the shower room, which was no better appointed than mine.

A doorway led from the kitchen into the bed-sitting room. Under the skylight, which was the only window in the apartment, there was a small desk with a chair tucked beneath it. On the desk was a spiralbound notebook with a number of pages missing (otherwise empty), a couple of cheap ballpoints, and a small, neat pile of three books – one of Simenon's Maigret stories, a Série Noire translation of a Robin Cook novel and *Djinn* by Alain Robbe-Grillet. They were standard paperback editions, not Braille. Elsewhere in the room there was a single bed, a dog basket, a free-standing radiator, a small chest of drawers and an armchair that needed re-covering. Behind the armchair was another door, glazed at the top, wooden panel at the bottom. The glass was covered over, but only on the other side. I dragged the armchair out of the way and tried the door handle. The door appeared to be locked. I inspected the top half more closely. There was a small hole in the covering on the other side of the glass. The hole was more or less at eye level. I approached the hole and peered through into my apartment – the bed, the nightstand, the round table in the middle of the room. You could see just about everything. It offered a very good view of the bed.

I pictured the half-glazed door from my side. The wallpaper on the glass. The hole must have been cut in the dark centre of one of the flowers.

I moved away from the door and repositioned the armchair. I sat down in the armchair. Faintly, I could hear the radio in my apartment. I looked around the room from where I sat. I wasn't looking for anything in particular. I noticed something I hadn't seen before, a little bedside table with something resting on it. I got up and walked across the room. From the bedside table I picked up the rubber eye mask. I turned it over in my hands. It had been hand-painted. There were little holes in the centre of the pupils that looked as if they had been made with a large-bore needle. I held the mask at arm's length and decided I could only see the holes now because I knew they were there. Besides, I had only ever seen the mask behind a pair of glasses.

I went to put the mask back down on the bedside table and saw that it had been resting on a piece of paper. I picked it up. It was a photocopied notice giving advance warning of a talk by Bernard Villemain at Université Paris V. The title of the talk appeared at the top of the page: 'Falcony and the Oedipus Complex: the Psychology of the Lure'. It was in French; the translation is mine. There was a bit of blurb, which mentioned names and theories that were familiar to me: Freud, Lacan and the Gaze, Laura Mulvey and the Male Gaze.

The date was two weeks hence.

I replaced the notice on the bedside table and positioned the mask on top of it.

I stood in the middle of the apartment, thinking.

I knelt on the arm of the armchair and had another look through the spy hole into my apartment.

I walked into the kitchen and opened various drawers and closed them again.

I inspected the damage to the door.

I took a glass from a cupboard and filled it from the cold tap. I drank the water and placed the glass on the worktop next to a dirty knife.

I went back into the other room and sat down in the armchair to wait.

· THE NIGHTINGALE ·

Jane and I had been to our favourite restaurant on the city's West Side, a little Korean place that somehow managed to position every table in a corner. It was good because it was the first place we went that was neither mine nor hers, nor was it Tessa's – my ex.

Jane and I had only been together a couple of weeks when Tessa remembered about giving me a hard time. How she let her resolve slip for a fortnight I didn't know, but I was counting my blessings and praying for the situation to last.

Some of it had been her doing and a lot of it mine. At first. I'd take Jane somewhere and halfway through the starter I'd remember being there with Tessa, and Jane would know instantly. 'Your face changes,' she used to say, and I could believe it. I could tell you all about Tessa and just what went wrong but there's no real need. Anyway, it's not a pretty story; nor is it extraordinary – how many couples think they've found true lasting love only to be brought back down to earth? Millions. It's happened to most people, it's probably happened to you. We share that much. But it's in what goes on afterwards that I hope we differ because I wouldn't wish my experience on anybody.

Basically, I'd promised Tessa the earth and she'd grabbed at the chance, giving up a great deal for it in terms of stability and comfort. So when it went wrong – living in too small a space and neither of us quite expecting the full force of the grief she felt after leaving the last guy she lived with, and the hard time *he* gave *her* (and me) — I felt like all different kinds of shit. Truly I felt bad. I went out and got the wooden cross and a bag of nails and came back and handed them to her: 'Here you go, Tessa. I'm all yours and I deserve it.' And, although I didn't realise it at the time, she took the hammer and nailed me right up there without wasting a minute. She did a great job. Those nails took months to work loose; it was at least a year before I could find any enthusiasm for anything at all, never mind women. Through friends I met Jane, however, and it felt right again. No pressure, just laughs. We went to the places I knew, and had taken Tessa to, and some places Jane recommended because she'd been to them with some loser only weeks earlier. It worked up to a point, but it felt too much like chasing away the ghosts.

And then we hit on this Korean place that neither of us had been to before and it was there that it really clicked between us. Still no pressure, but more laughs. Just the right mix of leaning back into something comfortable and pressing forward to explore something new. Jane asked me what I did. I told her something with computers. I mean, it was the truth, if not the whole story. I had to earn a living and it wasn't easy then. The country was in a state and there were no handouts.

We sat there with our elbows on the table, dipping into our rice noodles and seaweed soup, scooping up the last of the fried prawns and knocking back Chinju beer. It was the beginning of a new stretch of road and the great thing was it didn't have to lead anywhere. We were just cruising with the windows down and the warm night breeze in our hair.

We had some great times back at my boxy little flat on the industrial edge of the city. With the window open we'd make love for hours to the ceaseless murmurings of some chemical plant and the mad twisted song of a nightingale that had recently taken up residence in a struggling sycamore behind my building. Afterwards we'd lie there in a tangle of sheets and Jane would watch the changing pattern of my screen saver on the machine at the other end of the room – I never switched the thing off in those days and the screen saver kicked in whenever the computer was left untouched for longer than ten minutes.

One night the phone rang while we were in bed and I said leave it, but the ring and the noise of the machine picking up the call were enough to knock out my desire. I lay next to Jane and listened as the machine clicked off, the caller having hung up.

The phone rang again and Jane felt my body tense.

'Relax,' she said. 'Perhaps you should answer it.'

'No way,' I whispered, as if the caller could hear me. 'I know who it is.'

Tessa had called me seven or eight times a week after the split. I was willing to be friends – hell, I *wanted* to be – but each time we talked she asked the same questions to which there were no answers. Or there *were* answers, but I'd repeated them so many times they no longer meant anything, even to me. The flat was too small, I wasn't capable of dealing with her mood swings, I was inadequate, a bastard, unreliable… all that shit. But she'd cry and scream at me and I'd feel a hand take a hold of my insides and twist so that my own voice rose and I became incoherent, in turn pathetic in my self-abasement and spluttering in terrifying rages. After she'd hung up on me mid-sentence I'd fling the phone down and storm round the flat punching the air and shouting abuse she'd never hear, however bad it got.

And then the phone would go again and it would be 'I'm sorry – I'm really sorry' and 'Yeah, me too, I don't want to argue'. Within two minutes reason would fly away again and we'd be screaming at each other. I came to dread the phone ringing. I jumped out of my skin whenever it did.

After I met Jane the phone was pretty quiet, mercifully. Until that night. The first two times I let the machine get it and there was no message. The third time I leapt out of bed and got there first. 'Hello, hello?' No one there. No sound of breathing. No hanging-up noise. Just nothing. So I hung up and it went again. It rang eight times in half an hour and it was already well past midnight. Each time there was no one on the other end. Or no one with the guts to say anything.

'Do you think it's her?' Jane asked. She didn't like saying Tessa's name.

The funny thing was, I didn't think it was her. However bad it had been, I couldn't imagine her doing this, not after so long. Unless she was sitting there surrounded by empty gin bottles, her hair all in disarray, her sheets knotted like mine but for a different reason.

The next night Jane was there again and the phone rang once. No one spoke to me when I answered it. The same thing happened two nights later and I had to unplug the phone just so we could get to sleep. The only reason I'd delayed taking such action was because I could hardly believe it was Tessa, or some other nuisance caller, and that left the possibility of a fault – which the operator assured me was out of the question – or some friend or relative in trouble and unable to get through.

We tried sleeping at Jane's but it was difficult. She shared a place with two lovely girls who kept terrible company and six times out of ten Jane would return home late at night to find some strange man lying in her bed because one of the flatmates had had a better offer. And, anyway, both Jane and I liked it at my place – she was becoming quite attached to the nightingale, and the hypnotic effect of the screen saver helped her get off to sleep – and I didn't like being made to feel alienated in my own home.

Because I couldn't face the inevitable failure I'd said to Jane I was too tired to make love but I wasn't and it was her who drifted off to sleep first. The phone was unplugged but I still worried about it. I watched it from across the room, changing colour as the screen saver cast different hues across the white plastic, and I half expected it to ring, unplugged flex and all. I remembered how at the end I'd used tiredness as an excuse to avoid sleeping with Tessa. She thought she wasn't attractive but, as I kept telling her, it had nothing to do with that. I felt permanently in debt. However much I gave she wanted more and I couldn't keep up with the payments. If I kissed her on the lips she wanted to be fucked to within an inch of her life and I just couldn't keep up, emotionally or physically. Exit desire, goodbye good times.

Jane wasn't like that, which was why seeing her seemed to be doing me so much good. The fact I'd had to cry off sex through tiredness was unimportant. Tessa was Tessa and Jane was Jane.

I stroked little wisps of hair away from her face, where the draught from her nostrils was causing it to flutter and tickle the tender skin under her eyes. She breathed deeply and her unlined face looked untroubled. Her eyes moved slowly under their lids, which still held traces of smudged eyeliner. What was she dreaming about? Her head shifted slightly on the pillow and I could see the dark line of her external drive edged with red on the back of her neck right up by the hairline. No problem there; sometimes the older external drives became inflamed through irritation. A small frown furrowed her brow and she muttered something through half-closed lips. For a second, as the skin above her eyes creased in confusion, she had a look of Tessa about her. Just a look and then it was gone. I turned over and went to sleep.

In the morning Jane woke first and touched me gently. Sadly, you don't get much change out of me first thing in the morning and I only grunted as I burrowed deeper under the duvet. Jane lay on her back with a light sigh, then I felt her get out of bed and head for the bathroom.

'What are you doing today?' she asked me later as I lay in bed pretending still to be asleep. She wasn't stupid.

I made some noise to indicate I hadn't heard.

'What are you doing today? Are you busy? Only I was thinking about lunch. I'm free.'

'I've got to work,' I said. 'I've got a contract on.'

It was true but I could have made time to see Jane at lunch if I'd wanted to. I kicked myself. The week had started badly and it was my fault.

After she'd gone I sat in the bath and puzzled over why I'd kept Jane at a distance since the night before. The trick of the light that made her look like Tessa was just that – an illusion, and a brief one at that. I felt an unfocused annoyance and remained slumped in the cooling bathwater for too long. I climbed out and shivered under the warm ceiling fans.

I fixed a coffee and strapped myself into the driving seat in front of the computer. I watched the screen saver for a moment as I sipped my coffee. The twirling threads and leaking colours could insinuate themselves into your head if you switched off your brain and watched them for more than five minutes or so. I'd downloaded the saver from Tessa's machine via the phone lines. I'd just been looking at her stuff one day, browsing, as you do, through someone else's private files, and I came across the saver. It had no name, which suggested she'd obtained it by foul means over the wires from some technical craftsman in computerland. So I figured it was no more hers than anyone else's.

I nudged the mouse to clear the vivid tangle off the screen and double-clicked the icon where I'd hidden the work in progress. Kept on a secret partition of the hard disk it was inaccessible to pirates, unless they happened to be as good as my clients paid me to be. It was a short job but a lucrative one. I had to locate the accounts of an out-of-town hardware supplier and fiddle with them a little, not so as they'd notice, but enough to make them lose a major contract which my client wanted for himself. Kids' stuff but well paid.

I spent the morning running my cursor down columns of figures, altering a few vital numbers. It was easy enough, though important to alter the right amounts and essential not to remain patched through to the company's system for longer than 30 seconds at a time. I had to make several connections. In all, the job probably earned me two months' rent and took me seven hours to complete. From what I could see, the loss of the contract wouldn't cause any lasting financial damage to the supplier; not that such a consideration would have necessarily caused me to abandon the project, but I looked just to make sure.

Jane called on my personal line when I was halfway through and I was a bit short with her, which I regretted instantly, but the damage was done. I knew she was upset as she hung up. There had been a very slight speeding-up in her speech before she said goodbye.

It's easy to waste a whole afternoon kicking stuff around on screen, changing files, programming new savers, logging on to CompuServe. I had no problem. Seven-thirty, and Jane was due to arrive at eight. I rinsed the day's accumulated coffee cups and shaved. Jane didn't like kissing stubble. I wondered if I was beginning to find the compulsory shaving a drag. A few drops of rain rattled against the window and I heard the wind picking up. I thought about the first time Jane and I went out. We went somewhere, some restaurant in the heart of the city, and we talked a lot, but it was later that was important. She came back to my little flat and, although clearly we both liked each other's company, neither of us could depend on anything further to that. My confidence was at a low ebb. It was the kind of time when you're thinking every woman perceives you as a mass murderer and my flat, like any other, contained dozens of potential weapons. It was also one of those nights where you both sit there into the early hours not daring, either of you, to make a move, in case you screw up. We talked about family, friends, trips abroad, whatever. Anything except ourselves.

One of us said something and the light somehow flicked to green and we touched each other. We kissed, held each other, but didn't do much else. Being a bit sort of old-fashioned and cautious about it gave us a good start and a pretty good chance of it lasting more than a week.

I gave her a lift home while it was still dark, then, as I turned the car round and headed back east, the sun came up, pouring in through the windscreen. It felt like a blessing. I'd always thought, if you've got to believe in something, have some kind of deity to worship, why not go for the sun?

It comes up in your face, goes down on you at night – you can depend on it; which is more than you get with some old fucker with a beard who *still* lets 14-year-old kids die of cancer like he *still* didn't get the memo.

So it started well and the signs were good, though perhaps it was always going to go wrong. As if it was written into the script even then.

When she came round that night, after I'd been doing the hardware accounts thing, she was a little on edge – perhaps because of how I'd been with her on the phone – and I was wired. Too much coffee, hacked out. I had this funny feeling she was going to dump me just because I'd been weird with her.

We sat on the sofa with a couple of beers and watched the screen saver at the other end of the room. I felt it was up to me to say something but I had nothing to say.

I think I asked, 'You want to go out and eat?'

'Could do,' she may have replied.

Silence for a couple of beats.

Then I spoke: 'Seems more like you've come over here to say you don't want to see me any more.'

I turned to look at her and I swear I saw her face change – a lost, vulnerable and slightly bitter look fell across it, like a silk scarf draped across a bust. It made her look like Tessa. I looked away but in that instant I saw tics busying themselves in the skin beneath her eyes, tugging the face in different directions, changing the physiology as I watched.

'It won't be me who does it,' she said in a cracked little voice.

That's when it turned, with that remark and with the movement I'd seen in her face a moment before.

I asked her what she meant and she said that if either

of us was going to finish the relationship it would be me. I knew she'd had unsatisfactory relationships in the past and none lasting longer than a few months. Because ours had started well, she'd allowed herself to be optimistic.

There was a power shift that night that made me distinctly uncomfortable. She'd handed me the baton. I was clearly in control. Which would have been fine if that was what I wanted. But it wasn't. Hadn't been since Tessa. Ever since being in control meant hurting someone day and night.

I suppose I knew that night – perhaps we both did – that one day it would finish and it would be me who would do it, and from then on I began to see Tessa's features in Jane's face more and more. She was like a hologram; if I tilted her an inch she looked different. Also weighing me down was the sense of the injustice of it all: Jane was in fact nothing like Tessa; she looked and acted no more like Tessa than Mao Tse-tung, but she had the misfortune to be cast in the wrong role. No doubt she felt like an actress who takes over a major role after the star has had enough and gone on to do something else: the critics don't bother to come see the play again, so she carries the burden of her predecessor's bad notices.

There were some tears that night. I felt a bit shitty despite the fact I hadn't yet done anything. In the morning we improvised a hasty breakfast and Jane went off to work. I sent through the word to my client, and he must have been happy as hell, because I saw zeros lining up in my personal account before I even broke for lunch.

In the afternoon I bummed around, backed up some top stuff on to floppies. I came across Tessa's disk and wondered for the nth time if I should stick it in the machine and take a look. She'd kept a dream diary when we were together.

It was a simple matter of sticking the disk in the external drive before going to sleep and remembering to eject it in the morning. I'd tried it too once or twice at her suggestion, but there was a huge risk attached which I wasn't too happy about. You get a bad nightmare, the disk contains a dormant virus – you're fucked. Scrambled brains. Not my bag. Tessa lived closer to the edge than I did. She liked the view.

It was an unspoken rule: we didn't look at each other's personal disks. But she'd left hers when she'd gone, and while I'd never taken a look at it, I hadn't trashed it either, as I guess I should have done.

I thought again about having a quick scan, but decided against it. Whatever the ethics of it, Tessa's was one head I didn't fancy getting into just then.

Still, I thought I'd just bang the disk in the machine and check the folders were still intact, no harm in that. And it was only because I did that, I think, that I found out what was going on. As soon as the disk snapped in and I heard the accompanying sound – the nightingale which I'd recorded one night in full song – a message flashed on the screen to the effect that an uninvited guest had gatecrashed the hard drive.

They'd gone, of course, flitted off like my nocturnal songstress, when I went in and had a look. And whoever it had been was clearly a professional, because they left no trace of their intrusion. No drawers left hanging open, data sticking out. The place was clean. You couldn't even smell them. A professional. As good as I was.

I checked the secret partition.

The fuckers.

They'd got in. Fuck knows how, but they'd broken down that wall. There was debris here, no mistake. You couldn't get in that deep *and* get out again without leaving a calling card. Trouble was there was no name on it. Obviously I thought of the hardware supplier, then of my client, but there was perhaps one other person who'd fancy her chances at breaking in, and who had a motive. Plus the fact the machine had just accepted her disk. It could have connected the intruder with the ID on the disk.

So Tessa knew about the hardware job. That didn't bother me so much – I didn't imagine she'd be so petty as to use that against me. It was the fact she'd broken in at all. How dare she? Computer rape. Even if she never used what she'd obtained, it was just the fact that she'd been there – like the burglar who ransacks your underwear drawer.

I didn't call her or attempt to get through to her system. Let her think either I didn't know she'd been around, or I didn't care. Instead, I spent the afternoon constructing fresh defences designed to keep out the Pentagon, MI6, even Tessa.

Jane came round that night. I thought it'd be a good idea to get out of the flat and go see a movie or something. I forget what we saw – some American comedy on new release. As we came out of the multiplex, Jane said she liked the bit where the husband entered his office to discover his secretary in a compromising position with the office cleaner. Funny – I'd been thinking how it was my least favourite part of the movie.

When we got back we went straight to bed. Jane lay propped up against the pillows staring at the screen saver while I went through the motions, distracted by an idea which had occurred to me. Jane didn't seem to be aware of me at all. Her glassy eyes just gazed into the never-ending tunnel on the screen.

I stroked her hair, my fingers hesitating over the lip of her external drive on the back of her neck. It was empty. Mine was too.

I drifted off and woke maybe an hour later. Jane was asleep, lying on her side facing towards me. Her face was in the midst of transformation: crawling with tiny tics. One by one, tiny squares of her skin flashed or changed colour or just seemed to disappear, as if someone had laid a sheet of graph paper over her features and was busy crossing off little squares.

Suddenly I had a startlingly clear vision of what was happening. To wake Jane would do no good. Nor would remote interception.

I slid out of bed, taking a last look at Jane's face. It was as if someone was altering a photofit of a wanted suspect, guided by a witness who kept changing his mind. Which was pretty close to what I thought was happening.

I threw on some clothes and left the flat quietly. The car started without any problems. She'd be expecting me to arrive over the wires, if at all, as a blip in her system – and that's what she'd be looking for. So a personal visit, I thought, would be more likely to take her by surprise. I pulled into a side street two blocks away and killed the engine. Advancing silently down the street on rubber soles I reflected on the irony of it all: the times I'd heard strange noises in my flat and wondered if she was coming to take some terrible revenge, and now it was me who was calling round uninvited in the middle of the night.

I knew the layout of her flat, and that, unless she'd moved it, the computer was in a little room one storey and several doors away from the street. I leaned carefully against the small square of glass in the door. It didn't give, so I dealt it a swift blow with my elbow, and it fell into the hall in several pieces. I reached in and worked the lock. The break-in was fairly silent and all over in thirty seconds.

I moved to the next door and tried it. It was not locked. Inside, with the second door pulled to behind me, I listened.

Nothing.

I headed across the room and started climbing the stairs. Sweat started to crawl from my hairline like enemy troops out of the jungle. I'd recognised a book I'd given her lying on the floor in the room below. Some novel I'd liked and so imagined she'd be bound to like too. It's funny how you can think that two birds, just because they happen to be flying at the same speed and altitude for a brief moment in time, always have done and always will. How quickly they dart away from one another and fly in alarmingly different ways.

I could hear her now, working through the night, singing her little heart out. I wondered when she slept, how she earned a living. I could hear the steady click of her mouse, the hum of the machine itself. My scalp tightened as I poked my head above floor level and saw her hunched over the monitor, her back to me.

Hoping that she wouldn't hear me because she was concentrating so deeply, I climbed the rest of the stairs and stood in the room. She worked busily, her hand twitching as it repositioned the mouse fraction by fraction. I was scared I already knew what she was doing.

When she leaned back slightly and ran her left hand through her hair I stiffened and flattened myself against the wall. I saw the red-edged external drive beneath her hairline. It seemed to be empty. But she bent back down to her task. Another eighteen inches to the right and I could see the screen.

Jane's face, full on, occupied one half of the screen, a palette of colours and selection of tools filled the other. Tessa used the mouse to choose a colour and then she nipped across to the left of the screen and clicked on one of the hundreds of tiny pixel squares that made up the image of Jane's face. Frozen to the spot, I watched her darken the area under the left cheekbone. Then she moved the cursor up to the iris of Jane's left eye and I let out an involuntary murmur.

She jumped an inch off the chair and arched round on shaky legs to confront me.

Now I could see what her head had been concealing: a second monitor to the left of the first. On it was an image of her own face, which she was using as a model.

She was shouting something at me, spitting out a tangle of words that I didn't even try to unknot. I was looking intently at the second screen, the one with her face on it. In addition to the face, the palette and tools, there was a window with a message asking if she was sure she wanted to delete the file.

Her words came through on a several-second delay. Standard abuse, frightened blistering attacks. Then something about how it was my fault: 'You helped yourself to the screen saver, you stupid fucker. How do you think I got into her head?'

She had only to delete the file with a single keystoke and Tessa would be nothing but a hard chip of guilt in *my* head. Loose strands of hair hung in the air as she dipped down towards the desk.

I got to her just before she reached the keyboard.

· THE BLUE NOTEBOOKS ·

After the snow melted, the redwings appeared. I would see two or three hopping about in the scrubby grass beneath the trees. If I approached, they would fly up into the lower branches, revealing the red flash under the wing, like a handbag clutched beneath the arm.

Since I had started making regular visits to the library, I would make sure my route took me through Fog Lane Park and Platt Fields. At the lake I would pause to watch the coots and moorhens among the mallards, tufted ducks and Canada geese. A lone heron stood on one leg on the shore of the island. An Egyptian goose sat plumply on a paving stone at the rim of the lake. Mentally, I gave each bird a tick.

I was pleased to be asked to contribute to the event at the library, which was being billed as a celebration, but that pleasure could only mask the pain I felt at the prospect of the library's closure. It would be for no more than three or four years while refurbishment took place, but even if it did eventually reopen, would it be the same building I had loved all my life, its internal walls lined with Hopton Wood stone, its joinery of oak and English walnut? Would they have 'fixed' the unique acoustics of Great Hall, where the scrape of a chair leg on the floor would either transmit as the faintest rustle or reverberate like a thunderclap?

As a young man, I applied for writer-in-residence posts. The ceaseless stream of rejection letters did nothing to dent my confidence that, one day, some grand institution would open its doors and I would be paid to sit and write all day and occasionally read at public events where respect would be measured by rows of rapt expressions and rising levels of applause.

In my spare time I would write or I would walk. I walked for miles, thinking about what I was writing, never dwelling on my condition. I was young and relatively lucky to have inherited Usher syndrome type 3 rather than either type 1 or type 2. Progressive blindness would set in, but perhaps not until early middle age. I walked by rivers and along dismantled railway lines. I entered industrial zones and crossed waste ground. I found myself drawn to disused buildings – old hospitals, abandoned factories, where the whisper of fallen leaves across a concrete apron would effectively repopulate an empty space with the ghosts of the people who had once worked there or stayed there or lived there and died there. The movement of shadows in distant corners could be explained by the passage of the sun across the dome of the sky, but there was always the suggestion of something not so easily accounted for.

Pigeons became my closest companions. Magpies, jackdaws, a murder of crows. A murmuration of starlings. Tits – blue, great, long-tailed. The jenny wren. Birds that haunted the waste lands.

In a long-abandoned factory complex hard by the shell of the former Barnes Hospital, just off the A34, I was far from the first writer to have explored the grounds since their having fallen into disuse. Tet, Solb, Stum and many others had all been there before me, leaving their tags and pieces and throw-ups on the brick walls and great rusty gas cylinders. I dragged a dirt-ingrained desk and a broken-backed chair into the centre of a large room with no ceiling where Solb had written that he was 'INHALIN CHEMICALS' and took out my notebook and pen. There I was, writer-in-residence of Cheadle Bleach Works.

When you stand in St Peter's Square in front of the library and look directly at it, even a healthy eye is deceived. You are puzzled by its contradictions. The building is round, the entrance squared off, a two-storey portico with its six huge columns, four round and two square. The unusual colonnade around the second and third floors. The great dome that is not a dome.

My tunnel vision meant that if I looked above the main entrance, I couldn't see the empty plinths either side of it. A year earlier I had been able to.

I walked around the east side of the building and entered the loading bay that staff knew as Van Dock – as important a part of the library as Great Hall or Stack. I explained my business to the man at the little window, pointed to a yellow Post-it note on which his colleague had recorded my name and the number of the key I was permitted to borrow. I walked back around to the main entrance and took the stairs to the first floor, glancing at Ciniselli's *Reading Girl*, a blur in white marble on the half-landing. The issue desk at the top of the stairs was empty in preparation for closure. I turned left past Local Studies, climbed to the second floor and went left again. Affixed to the wall next to a room offering Services for Visually Impaired People was a bronze bas-relief of a man's profile. A plaque identified him as George MacDonald, poet, novelist and preacher, in gold lettering almost worn away from the fingertip searches of blind people. I passed the Chinese Library, the Training

Room, the Committee Rooms. On the right side of the corridor were the study carrels that had been turned into offices. I stopped before one of these, inserted my key in the lock, closed the door behind me and breathed out.

There hadn't been anybody following me, of course, but tunnel vision can make you paranoid.

Inside the room, there was a light switch but no light. Illumination was provided by a translucent skylight. A desk, two chairs, a large reinforced case, ten files tied with white ribbon and dated 2007. A reconstructed nineteenth-century box camera on castors that was being used by university photographers to document the library's secret spaces – Stack, the staff-only lift, the original Language and Literature Library.

I plugged in my laptop, arranged my things – diary, room key, my paperback copy of Agatha Christie's *The Body in the Library* with Tom Adams' painting of a dead girl's foot on the cover. I hadn't read Agatha Christie in thirty years, but the title had given me an idea for my story, a locked-room mystery called 'The Library in the Body'. I picked up the book, which I had read with some difficulty the week before.

There was a marker on page thirteen.

'*We've just found a body in the library,*' I read out loud, surprised by the sound of my voice. It had sounded as if somebody else was speaking.

The dialogue continued.

'*You've found a what?*'

'*I know. One doesn't believe it, does one? I mean, I thought they only happened in books.*'

I smiled at the self-referentiality.

I turned to my next marker. A young boy asks a policeman if he likes detective stories.

'*I do,*' the boy says – and again I was reading out loud, '*I read them all and I've got autographs from Dorothy Sayers and Agatha Christie and Dickson Carr and HC Bailey.*'

Who would have expected such postmodern trickery from Agatha Christie? In 1942. Had she perhaps read Cameron McCabe's *The Face on the Cutting-Room Floor*, published five years earlier, the narrator of which is a film editor called Cameron McCabe? And how amusing that she placed herself second in the list. To put herself last would have been dishonest; second to last, coy; first, arrogant.

I opened my laptop and stared at the blank screen. I looked around at the box camera, the reinforced case, the beribboned files. I began typing. I increased the size of the type until I could read it. I typed for ten minutes, only stopping when the tolling of the hour from the Town Hall clock interrupted my concentration. I reread what I had written, speaking the words in a murmur, then selected all the text and pressed delete. I sat back and listened to the noises of the library around me. Outside the office, two women had stopped for a chat. In half-whispers they discussed a colleague. I could only catch the odd word. Maybe the progressive deafness, which was supposed to keep pace with the vision loss, was finally accelerating.

I closed the laptop and moved the table a few inches, then climbed on to the chair and stepped on to the table. I reached up and released the catch that secured the skylight. It didn't open very far, but I could see the curved brickwork of the third floor. I want to call it the inner outer wall, or the outer inner wall, neither of which makes any sense at all unless you can see it, which I still just about could.

A clatter of wings made me cover my face. A pigeon, most likely. I retreated.

Taking the key, I left the room. I walked as far as the stairs. I wanted to go up. In my youth, I had haunted the Language and Literature Library on the fourth floor. It had been moved to the first floor within the last few years. A sign read, 'No public access beyond this point'. I started to walk up. On the third-floor landing a window gave me what would have been a good view of the real dome, hidden inside the false one. I stepped closer to the window. Between the base of the dome and the vertical curve of the brick wall – like a daredevil motorcyclist's wall of death – I could make out a progression of humped features: the skylights of the study carrels. Right next to one of them – maybe my own, I couldn't tell – was a mound of unidentified material. An abandoned coat? A pile of books? A stunted buddleia?

I turned and walked back down to the second floor and then on to the first. I entered the new Language and Literature Library, located certain titles, then crossed Great Hall, raising my head to appreciate the fall of light from the oculus – or eye – at the top of the dome, and detoured to the general readers' library, before returning to the second floor. Again, the feeling of being followed down the green-carpeted corridor.

I placed my books on the desk – short story collections by Sean O'Brien and Christopher Fowler, Thomas Ligotti, Jorge Luis Borges – and opened the laptop. The file was open and I saw with surprise that the text I had deleted remained onscreen. I reread it slowly. It still didn't work, but the last paragraph puzzled me most of all, because I didn't remember writing it. It didn't fit with the rest. I deleted all the text and pressed save to make sure.

A strange sound intruded on my consciousness, a pitter-patter, like faint applause. I looked about me, but the sound was coming from above, from the skylight. It had started to rain.

I turned to the books. I read 'The Library of Byzantium' by Ligotti, Fowler's 'Dracula's Library', 'The Library of Babel' by Borges, in which I smiled at the narrator's assertion that it's enough for a book to be possible for it to exist. And if it exists, it can be found in the Library, which we are told represents the universe. 'Only the impossible is excluded. For example: no book is also a stairway, though doubtless there are books that discuss and deny and demonstrate this possibility and others whose structure corresponds to that of a stairway.' I was reminded of my unwritten locked-room mystery, 'The Library in the Body', in which I imagined the discovery of a body in an unknown, empty building. A post-mortem examination would reveal the existence, within the anatomy, of stairways and corridors, shelves of books, their spines forming actual vertebrae. The body would have only one eye – or oculus – which would be wide open. The other eyelid would be sunken and closed over an empty socket.

At home, I tried to work on the story, but it wouldn't come. I had to be there. I had to be in the library. I looked out of the window. A pair of dunnocks was nesting in the garden. I had seen one of them every day for a week. I watched as it shuffled along close to the edge of the lawn. As a child I had never seen a dunnock. I tried to remember when I had seen my first one but couldn't. That was what my blue notebooks were for.

The blue notebooks were shelved together under the window. I took one down. In 1994 I had seen kittiwakes and puffins at the Farne Islands, a year later my first peregrine falcons in the Scottish Highlands. Now, they had moved into the cities. Recent years had seen them nest on tall buildings in Manchester and Salford. I closed my eyes and pictured the pair I had seen in the Highlands, mounting a fierce attack on a predator – unidentified, possibly an eagle – that had come too close to their nest. They had killed the larger bird, which had fallen out of sight.

I put the book back and pulled out the most recent. A fieldfare in Fog Lane Park, ring-necked parakeets in the same location. A brown shrike on Staines Moor, an extraordinary sighting.

I returned the blue notebook and looked at the walls of my own library, but it was like staring down the wrong end of a telescope. I went to the shelves and ran my fingers over the spines, immediately recalling a line from another Borges story about letterless books. I found the book it was in – the story is called 'August 25, 1983' – and started to read. The narrator – Borges himself – approaches a hotel where he will find his older self in the act of committing suicide. 'I felt, as on so many occasions, the relief and resignation inspired by places we know well,' he writes. I skipped forward to find the line I wanted. The older Borges says to the younger Borges, 'The misfortunes to which you have grown accustomed will keep on happening. You will live alone in this house. You will touch the letterless books…' It was his way of telling him how far his blindness would have progressed.

I remembered an earlier, similar story, 'The Other', and reached for another volume. In this story the older Borges tells his younger self that gradual blindness is not so bad. 'It's like a slow summer dusk,' he says. In the later story, he writes, 'Blindness isn't darkness – it's a form of loneliness.'

I knew that yet another collection contained a third

story in which the author again confronted the subject of his double – 'Borges and I' – but as I was reaching for my copy I noticed a tiny movement at the other side of the room.

There was a small bird on my desk and just enough light from the window to identify it as a dunnock. The pinkish legs and blue-grey face. I looked towards the window, which was shut tight, and then back at the desk – but the bird was no longer there.

In the morning, crossing Wilbraham Road, I was almost run over, my refusal to use a stick perhaps to blame.

I stumbled, shaken, into Platt Fields and sat by the lake. As my heart rate returned to normal I ticked off a Muscovy duck, a pochard, numerous mute swans and a large flock of lapwings, flickering black and white as they flapped lazily and silently over the water. My heart rate began to rise once more. Lapwing numbers had been declining for years, having been common in my youth, although never in an urban area such as this.

As I looked back while walking away from the lake I saw a large black bird soaring above all the others. It had the wingspan and wedge-shaped tail of a raven, the unmistakeable cruciform silhouette.

In St Peter's Square, a murmuration of starlings performed acrobatics in the sky above the library. A common sight in certain parts, but only at dusk.

I collected the key, then climbed the stairs to the first floor, suspicion hardening in my mind. In Great Hall, I asked at the counter and they directed me to the medical dictionaries. A scatter of redwings, clutching their scarlet handbags, cleared a path in front of me and flew up into the glare of the oculus. Charles Bonnet syndrome, I read, had been known to occur in a small number of cases in combination with Usher syndrome. Sufferers, in good mental health but with visual impairment, would experience complex, vivid hallucinations. I allowed the book to fall to the desk, triggering explosions of sound that ricocheted around the room, as I made my way to the stairs. The green-carpeted corridor on the second floor bristled with falcons: merlin, hobby, kestrel. A red kite soared noiselessly, the angle of its forked tail changing as it steered, wings unmoving. I unlocked the door to Room 10 and closed it behind me.

I unpacked my bag. The laptop. *The Body in the Library*. The Borges collections and the Sean O'Brien. Wasn't O'Brien's 'In the Silence Room' a locked-room mystery? I crossed to the door and locked it. I sat down, thinking of my blue notebooks, the records I had kept over many years, most of my life. What were they worth now? The kittiwakes and puffins, the fieldfare, parakeets and brown shrike. Had I seen any of them? The peregrine falcons defending their nest. I thought of the bundle by the skylight, glimpsed from the third floor. Could it be? Was it? I remembered the bird that had attacked me, which I had presumed to be a pigeon, perhaps wrongly. I thought of the high buildings in the city, the nesting peregrines. Was the library tall enough?

I stood on the table and opened the skylight. Something – the contact with cold air, or like Borges described, in his story about suicide, a feeling of relief and resignation – made my eyes film over with water.

· LOVEBITES ·

There had been a lot of rain during the past two weeks, it was true, but Joe only realised how much when he took the train to London. Looking out of the window between Stockport and Macclesfield, he saw tiny streams that were close to breaking their banks. It wasn't as if he had a photographic memory and knew what levels were normal for these watercourses, but a swollen river is a swollen river. You can tell just by looking at it. It looks too busy, the currents elaborately braided, like Jan's hair, he thought, on their wedding day.

He had, in fact, noticed that the Medlock had been higher than usual as he'd walked up Oxford Road two days earlier and happened to glance down through the perspex panel in the parapet where the road crossed the river at the same point that the railway bridge spanned the road. Most days the Medlock was a scrawny, straggly stream in an oversized canyon bound by tall buildings, like an old man's shrivelled neck in a loose shirt collar from younger days.

He instinctively raised a hand to his polo neck. Recent photographs had revealed signs of ageing on his own neck, a rippling craquelure caught by the camera's indifferent gaze. Admittedly he'd been turning his head to one side, but still. He'd reached for the polo-neck sweater almost every day since seeing that. But it was autumn, almost winter.

Turning away from the window, he looked around the carriage. The typical prohibitive signage of everyday life:

don't do this, don't do that. Doing this will attract a fine, doing that could land you in prison. A recently added sticker advertised the newly installed wifi hotspot. 'Fast, reliable, wireless internet. Log on now.' No mention of the charges he knew were levied, in spite of its being free in first class.

He looked back out of the window. Four horses in a field, all tightly packed in one corner in a defensive formation. Three standing, two sandy-coloured, one black, the fourth, also black, resting. All of them in a little group right in the corner staring in the same direction.

Another river running fast and close under a bridge of wooden planks.

Another field, four more horses. All four were standing, heads down, tearing at the long grass, each one angled away from the next. Go figure, as Jan would have said.

'Why you?' she'd said to him. 'Why do you have to go? Why couldn't they send someone else? What are you, an expert, all of a sudden?'

Well, yes. He was.

The train stopped at Stoke. Joe looked at a line of people standing outside the university building across the road stealing glances at one another, their hands mechanically rising to their mouths, fingering their lips. At the end of the line nearest the building's entrance, one man appeared to be resting his head on a female colleague's shoulder as if whispering in her ear.

Because of global warming, the temperatures in the Galapagos Islands, as everywhere else, were starting to rise. This didn't directly affect the vampire finches any more than they were already inconvenienced by the hot weather and parched conditions, driven as they always had been to peck at the skin of larger birds to draw blood to quench their thirst.

Five horses in a field. Four of them standing in a line, one wearing a coat over its back, all staring away from the train towards the far side of the field, the fifth angled away from the group, pointing in the direction of travel, head down, eating.

It was on the boobies that the rising temperatures had a direct effect; they were the birds on which the finches feasted. The booby can handle it hot, but not that hot, and numbers already seemed to be declining. If booby numbers were down, finches would follow, and before you knew it a chain in the ecosystem would have snapped. What next? Boobies, finches, giant tortoises, man?

'But why you?' Jan had repeatedly asked. 'Why can't they send someone without responsibilities?'

Who didn't have responsibilities? Especially now. Now it was almost too late.

Twenty-four black cows in a field, chewing grass, stretched out in a line across the green expanse like police officers. A fingertip search for a missing child.

Earlier in the week they had tried to have 'the conversation' with Cal. One they'd known they could not put off much longer. At 12 he was growing up fast, exposed on a daily basis to all sorts of pressures. *Here, try this. Do that. Have a go on this.*

All the parents they knew with older children had been through it. The crisis of hypocrisy.

'Cal,' Jan had said. 'We don't want to be telling you not to do things all the time.'

'But there are certain things we won't allow,' Joe had said.

'Yeah, yeah.' They didn't need to spell it out.

'It's important, Cal.'

'Anyway,' Cal had said. 'I don't want to. I've always said. It doesn't appeal.'

'You'll come under a lot of pressure.'

'It's stupid. It's bad for you,' Cal had continued.

'Of course it is. But when you're this age and you're hanging out with friends, down the park, on the street, sooner or later someone will offer…'

'And I'll say no.'

'We'd know, you know. We would know. It'd be on your clothes, on your breath. It's a dead giveaway and it's a killer.'

'I know, I know.'

Did he know? Did he really know? Joe had known, but it hadn't stopped him. Or Jan, in her day. When they'd got together it had been touch and go whether they would stay together, and it had had a lot to do with whether she could quit. For Jan, he suspected, the desire had never gone away. He came home sometimes and found her standing outside. Or she'd be indoors but her skin would be cold to the touch and she would have flushed cheeks and minty breath.

Joe supposed pigeons were like people. Every time he came to London he was surprised by the sheer numbers of them – pigeons – but really it was the same in Manchester. Just that there were a lot more of them in the capital. Like people.

They got under his feet as he walked out of the station. Just like the human population down here, they were more prone to ignore you until you were wading through them like a tide of filth. The university was a tube ride away, but Joe was early and preferred to walk. He passed groups of people gathered outside buildings. Some turned to their neighbours, others lost in their own thoughts. In Fitzroy Square he saw a Japanese girl on a yellow bike. Every part of the bike, not just the frame. Wheel rims, tyres, even the spokes, brake levers and saddle – all yellow. Behind a bus shelter on Old Street, a pile of leathery orange plane leaves revolved in a series of trapped eddies. Outside a Shoreditch pub, a man and a woman clung to each other, mouths clamped to each other's necks. Across the street, the same scene was repeated outside an office block. Three couples biting each other's necks, a lone individual, his tie loose, top button undone, waiting. For his turn? For a colleague to arrive?

People having to leave offices and the workplace to partake – that was nothing new. But the extension of the ban to pubs and bars, places of entertainment, was still fairly recent. Back home, following his usual routes, he was used to the sight of office workers lining the pavement, drinkers trickling out of pubs in the rain, slaves to their habits.

'Nanny state,' Jan had complained.

'You of all people should be on board with it,' he'd argued.

'Because I nurse patients with blood disorders?'

'You're better acquainted than most with all the communicable diseases.'

'It's a question of freedom of choice, though, isn't it? It's not like it's going to stop anyone. They'll just go elsewhere. Outside.'

'What about Cal? What about "the conversation"?'

'We've made him aware of the dangers.'

'That's it? We don't strictly, expressly forbid it?'

'What did your parents do?'

'They strictly, expressly forbade it.'

'Did it stop you?'

'No.'

'Well then.'

'I don't know about you,' he'd said, 'but I'm much happier

going for a drink in a pub, or having a meal in a restaurant, since the ban.'

'Passive bleeding?' she'd scoffed.

'Spillages. Dirty clothes. The floors were disgusting. Sticky and slippery at the same time.'

Joe reached the campus where the conference was taking place. He did his bit, said his piece, shook everybody's hand and left.

Jan would ask him how it had gone. She wasn't interested in the progression of his career, just whether he would actually be sent to the Galapagos and if so for how long.

Two hours later he was back on the train heading north. There was a girl. Woman, girl. She looked about 23, but could have been younger. She was sitting one row in front across the aisle, so every time he looked up from the report he was writing on the plight of the vampire finch, there she was, right in his field of vision. She wasn't even his type. The bleached hair, the cheap beads, the leopard-print pumps. The lovebites he could see when she flicked her hair out of her face. She was a big girl, voluptuous, lots of black eye make-up. She read neither a book nor a newspaper. Every few minutes she scanned a text on her phone or played a game of patience, but mostly she just sat and stared out of the window. Whenever she shifted in her seat Joe watched the way her weight was redistributed. He found he liked the slight bulge of flesh over the black straps of her bra, which could be seen through the coarse knit of her white woollen top. He read and reread the same sentence, but kept looking up, hoping to catch her profile as she turned towards his side of the carriage. The soft swell under her chin, the downy hair at the back of her neck.

Every time she turned even halfway in his direction he looked down, even though what he wanted above all was to make eye contact. It was so hard to control one's instinctive reaction. But another instinctive reaction made it impossible to concentrate on his work. He closed the laptop and stowed it in his bag. The next time she looked around he managed to hold his stare. She gave a flicker of a smile, clearly aware that he'd been watching her. She moved her bulk around in her seat, favouring him with a more generous view. He moved also, trying to get comfortable. She raised a hand behind her head, lifting her hair away from the back of her neck and letting it fall again. He rubbed his chin.

She rummaged in her lap, looking for something in her handbag. A small pot of lip balm. She unscrewed the lid and inserted the second finger of her right hand and moved it around inside the pot. He imagined the contact of the tip of her finger with the greasy ointment within. He imagined the trail of tiny lines left by her fingerprints. Then she raised her finger to her lips and applied the balm. Upper lip, lower lip. She then repeated the action before screwing the lid back on to the pot and dropping it in her bag.

Joe pictured the arm movements of the people he had seen outside their offices, in the doorways of pubs. Applying vaseline, lip balm, moisturising lip gloss.

The girl's hand settled on the armrest. He watched her arm, for the slightest sign of tension in the biceps. The flesh tightened. She was getting up. She rose slowly to her feet, pulled her top down at the hem where it had become crumpled, and smoothed the creases away with deliberate slowness over the swelling tops of her thighs in their black leggings. As she stepped into the aisle, she turned halfway around and looked at Joe. He smiled up at her. She half-smiled back. An eyebrow rose by an immeasurable degree. She turned away and started walking down the aisle towards the end of the carriage. When the girl reached the sliding door and stepped through, Joe got up and followed her.

As he approached the sliding door he saw the light for the toilet switch from unoccupied to occupied. He passed beyond the sliding door and waited for it to close behind him before tapping on the toilet door. The door was opened and he slipped inside.

Only once before, he remembered, had he shared one of these toilets with another individual. A long-ago girlfriend on a day trip to London. He felt a familiar, intense excitement now. The girl stood in front of the mirror with her back to it, so that he saw himself as he approached her. In the old days, they had had windows in the toilets, with frosted glass, allowing natural light to flood the interior. Somehow the artificial light was both harsher and more erotic. He considered the swooping curves and tactile physicality of her body as he raised his hands to move her hair away from her face. She smiled nervously. He smiled back, breathing shallowly. Her lips were full and slightly parted, her teeth a little uneven, but clean, white.

From her handbag she produced the jar of lip balm. He took it and unscrewed the lid, applying a smear to his own lips and then, on impulse, returning his finger to the jar. She let him recoat her lips before taking the jar off him and putting it away.

As they kissed – her soft lips yielding until he could feel the hard resistance of her teeth – he moved his hands down from her face to the sides of her neck. His fingertips quested as if reading Braille. She pulled away. He opened his eyes, refocused.

'Look,' she said.

She pointed at the sign. NO BITING. PUNISHABLE BY LAW.

He smiled and gently but firmly grasped her face in his hands, turning it to the side so that her neck was exposed. Some of her lovebites were more recent than others. They only increased his arousal. He ran his lips over the tiny hairs on the skin of her neck until she shivered. His eyes opened briefly and saw in the mirror the reflection of the sign that prohibited biting. He thought about the dangers. He thought about HIV, hepatitis, scrapie, CJD. He thought about Jan. He thought about what they had said to Cal. He thought about the swollen rivers and the horses and the cows. He thought about the rain and the storms and the rising temperatures. He thought about the Galapagos and about the boobies and the vampire finches and he closed his eyes again in a kind of helpless swoon of surrender as he opened his mouth wide, grateful for the lip balm, and pressed his teeth into the flesh of her neck.

· THE CHILDREN ·

I met an older man in the restaurant. We were both queueing for swordfish at the self-service buffet. He was in his sixties, white hair, tan; I guessed he was an ex-racing driver or director of his own small IT company. Perhaps both.

'Just arrived?' I asked, aware that some guests had already been at the resort a week, having booked for two.

'Yes.'

'Early start?' I said. 'Our flight left at 5.15am.'

'There was a five-hour delay at Gatwick,' he said, with a rueful grimace. 'It's hard when you've got kids.'

Not *It must be hard when you've got kids* or *It's hard when you've got kids with you.*

It's hard when you've got kids.

Some men have kids in their sixties. I wondered how old their mother might be if he was indeed their father.

'It certainly is,' I said. 'Ours *loved* getting up at 2am to be at the airport for 3.15.'

He had reached the front of the queue and was now helping himself to grilled swordfish.

'See you later,' he said.

'See you.'

I got some swordfish for myself and a couple of pieces for Eleanor, then added salad and chips to both plates and headed into the seating area. Eleanor had got us a table just in the shade, which was good, as it was 36 degrees in direct sunlight. The children had gone straight to the kids' club.

'How much do you recognise?' I asked her.

'It's coming back to me,' she said.

We had been to the same place before the children were born, which had been a mistake, really, because the main draw here was the childcare.

All over the restaurant, which was open on three sides with a high ceiling, sparrows flew from one unoccupied table to another, balancing on the backs of chairs, eating crumbs off tablecloths.

'Now we know why sparrow numbers are down,' I said. 'They all came here. On holiday.'

After lunch, on our way to the bungalow to unpack, I saw the man from the restaurant. Swordfish Man. He was at the far end of one of the long paths that break up the accommodation area and provide access to the bungalows. His wife was with him and even at that distance, from her posture and figure, I could tell she wasn't much younger than he was, maybe five years, possibly ten. It was hard to put an age on their children. There were two of them, but they were too far away to see properly. He had a hold of one and she was pulling on the other. They appeared to be dragging their children along.

We unpacked and then Eleanor lay down for a nap, while I went out for a walk. I turned left out of the bungalow and strolled past a row of units that were identical apart from the colours of the doors. At the end I reached a Y-junction: left for the beach, right for the tennis courts. I took the right fork and walked past a line of empty green wire-mesh cages carpeted with AstroTurf. Banners advertising sports brands were hung on the dividing fences. In the last court, two women were playing, each grunting heavily as she struck the ball.

The hotel was situated on the left of the path, its laundry room hidden behind a line of pink-flowering oleanders, the accommodation block rising four floors above it. Beyond this was the entrance to the hotel lobby, a late twentieth-century construction of cool marble and plate glass. Instead of going inside, I walked past the hotel entrance, where a chalked notice on a blackboard announced 'manager's drinks' in the bar at 6.30pm. The kids' club was on the right and next to that a five-a-side football pitch. Beyond this, a gate led to a narrow lagoon. Washing was hanging out to dry at bungalows on the other side of the lagoon; these looked like staff quarters. Swallows swooped and dived, dipping their beaks to take flies and other insects from the surface of the lagoon.

Walking back towards the hotel entrance I saw a couple I had noticed on the plane. They were almost impossibly glamorous. He was tall and blond, his hair bobbed and curly in a way you would not expect a man to carry off, yet he did so with ease. His wife, who walked with a jaunty marching gait, was also blonde; she had already swopped her travelling clothes for a yellow polka-dot bikini. Eleanor had them down as a barrister and spouse, though which she thought was which she hadn't said.

I passed through the hotel lobby, where argumentative men lined up at the reception desk to complain about minor deficiencies in their rooms' fixtures and fittings, to the main bar area, which was outside, separated from the restaurant by a wooden trellis. At several tables, middle-aged men in short-sleeved shirts and flowery shorts sat with glasses of beer and day-old copies of the *Daily Telegraph*. I walked on towards the beach bar and then on to the beach itself. Coarse sand worked its way into my shoes. To the left were two long lines of fixed sun umbrellas; many of the sun-loungers beneath them had already been taken. I saw Swordfish Man crossing the beach to reach the line of sun umbrellas. He appeared to be half-dragging, half-carrying one of his children, a boy, to judge from the shape and size of him, who looked too big to be carried at all. Reaching the line of umbrellas, Swordfish Man propped the boy up on a sun-lounger facing the sea. The boy's head lolled and the man straightened it. I stood and watched for a few moments while Swordfish Man sat on the next sun-lounger and took out something that looked like a crossword or sudoku; the boy didn't move a muscle, just stared blankly out to sea.

I walked past the beach bar and took a different route back to the bungalow. This path, running in a straight line between the beach and the accommodation area, took me right past the volleyball court where, I saw, players were assembling for a game.

'Are you playing?' a bare-chested man asked me.

'No, I… Are you short?' I asked him.

'One short. Jump on this side with us.'

A girl in a white T-shirt bearing the logo of the holiday company that leased the resort finished watering the sand and coiled her hosepipe by the side of the court.

'Are you ready, guys?' she asked us.

I slipped my shoes off and the game began. Each point won was celebrated with high-fives and hand slaps. Points lost – at this early stage – either went unremarked or were met with a shout of 'Unlucky' or 'Right idea', but I sensed that if points were lost when they mattered more, failure would not be tolerated so patiently.

'Come on, guys!' someone behind me exhorted the team when I failed to jump high enough at the net and the ball rolled out.

'He rose like a tin of salmon,' said another and everybody laughed.

One man – a company director? A QC? – slapped me on the shoulder in a matey fashion.

As we played, the wind picked up and cumulonimbus massed ominously over the mountains to the north. When it was not obscured by passing clouds, the sun remained very hot. I kept my hat on.

We ended up losing the first game, but won the second and so went into the decider – passing under the net for a second time – with vigorous handshakes all round. The rep in the white T-shirt then caused some consternation by asking for the ball we had been playing with and offering one in its place that was clearly inferior.

Because our games had taken longer than normal, we had used up the time officially set aside for the game and the rep needed to go to her next timetabled activity. She had been told she had to return the ball to the manager's office, she explained. Too many good volleyballs had gone astray in the previous week, apparently.

A tall, well-built man called Gary had the ball, ready to serve, and he obviously intended to hold on to it.

'They're not having this back until we've finished,' he muttered.

Two or three similarly built men, uniformly tanned, stood around him, providing backup. They did not intend to let the rep take the ball. The stand-off didn't last long. The rep graciously withdrew, although not without asking for an assurance that someone would return the ball to the office after the game.

'Given what we're paying,' a man called Rich said to me, 'they can afford to buy a few new volleyballs, right?'

I nodded.

We played the game, recording a narrow win, and after the obligatory high-fives and unironic soul brother handshakes, I set off down the path parallel to the shoreline. It took me past the children's swimming pool, where, among the many parents-with-children, I noticed Swordfish Man's wife with, presumably, their daughter. The sun was in my eyes, but the young girl looked remarkably lumpy and incapable of independent movement. Her mother appeared to be dragging her towards the exit, her feet bumping over a discarded swimming float and bouncing with the apparent lifelessness of a dummy.

Reminded of my own children and checking the time, I switched direction in order to go and pick them up from the kids' club. We had been a little nervous of the children's reaction to being stuck in childcare, but we needn't have worried. As I walked back to the bungalow with them past the tennis courts – the grunting singles players had been replaced by a game of doubles, all four wearing dazzling whites – the children babbled excitedly about their instructors and their group leaders and the friends they had made during the afternoon.

At the bungalow, Eleanor was feeling refreshed; she had already changed for dinner. I ran a bath for the children while Eleanor got busy with the hair straighteners. Emily, our eight-year-old, seeing her mother walking to and fro past the bathroom door, asked if she could use the straighteners next. Her ten-year-old brother, Henry, strongly advised her against it.

'Of course you can't, stupid!' he said.

'Henry,' I admonished him gently. 'Why can't she?'

'Because if she drops them in the bath she'll *explode*!' he shouted, splashing water in Emily's face.

Emily, predictably, screamed and started crying. While comforting her and patting her face with a towel, I explained why it wouldn't be a good idea to use the hair straighteners in the bath.

'You wouldn't explode,' I said. 'But you would be electrocuted and it would almost certainly kill you – and Henry, if he was still in the bath. You must never use electrical equipment in the bathroom.'

Tearfully and in a surprisingly worldweary tone for a child of eight, Emily said that she knew all about that and that she had meant she wanted to use the hair straighteners after getting out of the bath.

'Oh,' I said, feeling simultaneously deflated and quietly impressed. 'OK.'

I left the children to finish in the bathroom and went and opened the French window at the rear of the bungalow. I stepped out on to the tiny square of tiled patio and looked at the grassy expanse that separated the line of bungalows from the beach. A random scattering of orange sun-loungers broke up the green monotony.

We reached the bar at about five to six. The wind had died down to a light onshore breeze and the mass of thunderclouds had disappeared.

'Five to six,' I said, looking wistfully at the drinks behind the bar.

'It's all right,' Emily said. 'You're on holiday. You don't need to wait until six o'clock when we're on holiday.'

As I waited to be served I watched the guests gathering in the bar area for 'manager's drinks'. I saw the Glamorous Couple with their two extraordinarily cute children wearing top-of-the-range catalogue-wear accessorised with appropriate articles borrowed from their parents' wardrobes for a faintly radical touch. I tried to spot the alpha males from the volleyball court, but dressed – in short-sleeved shirts and three-quarter-length trousers – and without their sunglasses they would have looked completely different.

Swordfish Man and his family were sitting furthest away in an isolated spot, closest to the beach; I could see four drinks standing on their table.

The pool, which was situated between the bar/restaurant area and the beach, was absolutely still, like a giant glacier mint. A notice said that it was closed at 5pm each day.

Emily and Henry wandered into the hotel lobby to play table tennis; Eleanor and I selected a table and sat down with our drinks.

At breakfast, we watched as a steady stream of guests, mainly women, passed by the pool on their way to the restaurant in order to place towels on sun-loungers. The resort manager had made a specific request at 'manager's drinks' the night before that sun-loungers not be reserved in this way. He had even made a joke about us not being Germans and everybody had dutifully laughed. But his message, it seemed, had fallen on deaf ears.

The children went to kids' club and Eleanor went to a Pilates class. I said I was going to sit in the restaurant for a while and read my book. I did stay and I had another cup of mint tea, the Lipton's being undrinkable, but I didn't get much reading done. I watched the birds instead. While the sparrows made short, purposeful journeys in straight lines, the swallows – which had built three mud nests adhering to the top of the rear wall close to its junction with the roof – swooped in under the canopy and followed a curved path upwards to their nests, from which they then turned away at the last second to perform another low pass over the occupied tables in the middle of the restaurant before dive-bombing the swimming pool, performing a turn over the beach and returning for another acrobatic display above the heads of those guests lingering over croissants or the chef's peerless poached eggs. Their tireless description of curves and parabolas made their flight seem an expression of joy. I sat and watched them for so long that by the time I left the restaurant and joined the path next to the volleyball court, the 11 o'clock game was preparing to start. The rep asked me if I wanted to play, but a quick headcount told me the sides were equal and adequate in number, and I didn't hear any encouragement from any of the players on the court, so I shook my head, smiled from behind my sunglasses and walked on.

Ahead of me, crossing the path on a diagonal line from the bungalows to the beach, was Swordfish Man. He was carrying one of his 'children' and pulling the other behind him. He looked up and saw me and I offered what was meant to be a smile of recognition and fellow feeling but probably appeared as a caught-you-out smirk, because he did not return it, just muttered something unintelligible to his squashy burden and carried on towards the line of fixed sun umbrellas. I watched him go, dumping the 'children' on a couple of sun-loungers before pulling his T-shirt off over his head and walking towards the sea.

I sat on my own further down the beach and tried to get into my book, distracted this time by the unmistakeable silhouette in the sky directly above me of a corvid. An inability to judge scale, however, meant I wasn't sure if it was a crow or a raven. On a beach in England you would expect neither; maybe ravens were commoner here? I must have dozed off because I woke with a start and a strange taste in my mouth. The black bird was still circling and had been joined by another. My book had fallen to the sand. I raised myself on to my elbows and shielded my eyes to look down the beach, but couldn't see Swordfish Man or his family. The warning flags on the lifeguard's tower, which had been hanging limp before, were fluttering now in a light breeze. The day's weather was following the standard pattern. The wind would increase throughout the afternoon and clouds would build up in the north-west.

By mid-afternoon there was a rumble of thunder. The storm was fifteen or twenty miles away, but the staff were taking no chances and closed the pool. The bar, where I was sitting with my book, suddenly filled up with people in states of semi-undress. Half an hour later, when no more thunder had been heard, the pool was reopened and even though there was less than an hour until its normal closing time, it filled up again quickly.

The days followed a similar pattern and became indistinguishable from each other. Had we only been staying for a week, the calendar would have been fixed. At one end, the day of arrival and a couple of days following it, at the other our departure date casting its shadow backwards into the latter half of the week. But as we were staying for a fortnight, the calendar became fluid. It melted in the heat. Each day was the same as the next and the one after. That was what you paid for, the illusion of eternity in paradise.

Every day, by breakfast time it was already extremely warm and it would remain still and get hotter throughout the morning. The wind, getting up around lunchtime, brought relief from the heat and gathered strength throughout the afternoon, pleasing the sailors and windsurfers. The build-up of clouds, the booming timpani of a distant storm and the consequent threat of a pool closure would introduce a whisper of tension into a general atmosphere of tranquil relaxation.

As the clouds finally disappeared, calm would settle over the resort. People would return from their activities, shower, change, drift back to the bar in smart leisurewear. They would dine in one of three on-site restaurants and gravitate back to the bar for the evening's entertainment, whether it be the kids' club show, the prize-giving ceremony, the staff revue or boutique fashion show. And the main bar would slowly empty as the beach bar gradually filled up with the older teenagers, taking full advantage of the relaxed licensing arrangements and their parents' liberal attitudes. By morning, the volleyball court would need to be cleared of plastic glasses and cigarette ends before the new day could begin.

One afternoon a sudden squall emptied the pool faster than the lifeguards had been able to during the previous precautionary closure. There was no thunder or lightning, but the fat summer rain fell like a torrent of ball bearings. Amid squeals and screams, the sunbathers scattered, rescuing celebrity autobiographies, succeed-in-business primers and Patricia Cornwell novels.

'There goes Tennis Woman,' Eleanor said to me, having just returned from a stretch class. 'Running for cover.'

Tennis Woman was always the first in the pool area with her towels in the morning – all five of them – despite the fact that she and the rest of her family would spend most of the morning playing tennis. Well into her fifties, Tennis Woman kept the weight off with a diet of tennis and cigarettes, but her parchment-like skin collected in wrinkled pouches at key areas; her husband, a handsome watersports enthusiast, did not play volleyball but was always very relaxed around those who did. I had not played again following my first, disappointing attempt.

'And there's Swordfish Man,' I said, pointing to the gap between the main bar and the beach bar where a figure could be seen struggling with a heavy load, making his way from the line of fixed sun umbrellas towards the accommodation area.

'I feel sorry for him,' Eleanor said.

'I wonder how far they take the pretence,' I said. 'Do you suppose they paid for them to come here, for example?'

A black-and-grey bird alighted on the roof of the beach bar.

'What's that?' Eleanor asked.

'A hooded crow,' I said.

'Are you having a nice time?' she asked.

'I am,' I said. 'The longer we are here, though, the more I dissociate from real life, from normality.'

It was true. I found I was losing the capacity to care about things. About my book. About people.

'I spend hours just watching the birds,' I said.

The following afternoon brought another flurry of rain and as thunder could be heard in the distance the lifeguards closed the pool, interrupting a game of water polo. The players gathered in the bar, their floral shorts dripping over the deckboards. Large frosted tankards of beer appeared in meaty hands and bottles of wine lolled in ice buckets. Water polo and volleyball were timetabled on alternate days and tended to attract many of the same participants, mostly male.

The rain cleared up, but the pool remained closed, even after the half-hour mark. One of the holiday reps appeared with a blackboard, which she leaned against the wooden pillar close to the entrance to the pool. Kneeling down, she began to write on it in chalk.

'BAD WEATHER ACTIVITIES,' she wrote and then, above that, in red chalk, 'POOL CLOSED!'

She went on to compile a list of those activities that were still taking place. The exercise classes – yoga, Pilates, core abs – were run on concrete platforms under protective awnings, and on rubber mats, too, so were considered quite safe. The happy hour was brought forward, but the guests in the bar – the water polo players, volleyballers, swimmers and those who had been working on their tans – were not happy. Instead of rumbles of thunder, grumbles of discontent could be heard. Tennis Woman's husband approached the kneeling rep and asked why the pool was still shut since the sun was out again and the puddles of water around the bar were already evaporating. The rep's reply could not be heard, but she pointed towards the mountains in the north-west, where there was still an adumbration of dark cloud.

The rep returned to the hotel lobby, leaving her blackboard to guard the entrance to the pool. Eleanor appeared by my side and together we watched as the men in the bar finished their beers and Tennis Woman upended a bottle of wine over her glass. There was a restlessness, an electricity that had little to do with the thunderclouds over the mountains. The men were murmuring. Tennis Woman sucked long and hard on her cigarette, which rustled like an unseen bird in undergrowth. The sun had gone in again, but the air remained sticky and close. The men started clapping each other on the back, high-fiving, egging each other on. I spotted Gary, who had been intent on hanging on to the best volleyball at the beginning of the week, emerging through the group, taking the lead. He was the first one through the gate, but the others followed close behind. One by one, they dived in. Tennis Woman stubbed out her cigarette and rushed to reclaim her sun-lounger.

Eleanor tapped me on the arm. I turned to see the Glamorous Couple enter the bar. She was in her yellow polka-dot bikini, he was wearing a pair of bright green shorts that looked unfashionably brief but had probably cost more than my entire wardrobe. They watched the men pouring into the pool, above which the sky was darkening. He happened to look across at us and catch my eye. I raised an eyebrow and he half-smiled in reply.

The rep came running out of the hotel lobby, shouting that the pool was closed and that everybody had to get out. Of those who had re-entered the pool, no one paid any notice. Those of us remaining in the bar watched intently, as if the evening's entertainment had begun early. The rep bobbed back into the hotel lobby to call for backup and then returned to the gate, but she found it held fast on the other side by one of the biggest, strongest volleyball players. Gary, it looked like, or possibly Rich.

The rep's backup arrived – bar staff, several male holiday reps, tennis coaches and sailing instructors, even the nightwatchman. But there were so many men now in the pool, all of the volleyball players, the water polo crowd, those who had been sailing and windsurfing, that the staff held back. Tennis Woman sat upright on her sun-lounger, cigarette hanging out of the corner of her mouth, clapping her liver-spotted hands in glee as her husband joined the thrashing throng in the pool.

Heads down, the staff discussed their options and appeared to settle for the easiest one; they turned to face the bar and asked us all to leave. Amid half-hearted resentful remarks that if anyone deserved to be bossed around it was not us, we all slowly got up and started to shuffle out of the bar.

'Go to your rooms, guys,' the staff shouted over the din from the pool. 'Show's over.'

'Happy hour from six,' called a member of the bar staff. 'Come back then, guys.'

As we left the bar and headed away from the hotel on the path by the volleyball court, I saw how much darker the sky had become. The air was uncomfortably hot and there was a strange, dead quality to objects in the landscape. The fixed sun umbrellas, the volleyball net, the lifeguard's tower – all these familiar artefacts suddenly appeared unfamiliar, as if dangerous or unreal. They seemed to have no stronger connection to reality than the amorphous blobs in the nightmarish paintings of Yves Tanguy.

And then suddenly, for less than a second, the beach and its contents were lit up, starkly outlined, as if someone had come along with a camera and the flash had gone off. A second or two later, an ear-splitting peal of thunder seemed to squeeze the still, viscous air around us almost to bursting point. Most of those people on the path actually crouched down or at least bent at the knee in an instinctive response to the force of the detonation.

When the next strike arrived, everything happened at once. There was an extraordinarily bright flash of light, its source somewhere very close behind us, and at the same time an instantaneous series of explosions, like a piano falling downstairs or boxes of fireworks going off one after another, and a terrifying hissing, spitting sound unlike anything I had ever heard before. But I knew exactly what it was the moment I heard it and I think everybody around me did, too.

For several seconds no one dared turn around and the silence was like the silence you read about in newspaper reports and hope never to hear, the silence that follows the impact of a plane crash, the silence that will be broken only by the first moans or screams as consciousness finally catches up with the speed of actuality.

But as one or two of those on the path started to walk back towards the pool, still nothing could be heard. Neither cries of pain nor the sound of footsteps. The thunder had deafened me. Was this merciful? Were there terrible sounds to hear? Had anyone at all survived the lightning strike? Was Tennis Woman frozen in shock on her sunbed as she stared at the snapshot from Hell that I imagined the pool had become?

I didn't know and, worse than this not-knowing, I found I didn't care.

As others moved past me back towards the pool to bear witness, I stopped and looked at the path. By my foot was a small, blackened thing. I stooped to pick it up and its feathers felt crispy against the pads of my fingers. Some charring speckled the white breast, the red throat. It weighed nothing in my palm. The twin spikes of the tail were like scorched needles.

I walked away from the pool, the bar area, the volleyball court. If Eleanor called after me, I didn't hear her. I continued to walk down the path towards the accommodation area. After passing the empty children's pool on my left, I turned away from the beach, on to the grassed area that many of the bungalows looked out on to. My eyes scanned the backs of the units, each with its French window and small patio, plastic chairs and drying rack for wet clothes. The dead swallow shifted within my closed left hand and I felt something building inside me, moving from my stomach to my throat, a sense of pressure, like mercury rising.

Third from the left in the furthest group of bungalows I saw a family group sitting out on their plastic chairs. Mother, father, two children. One of the children – the older one, the boy – was slumped over the side of his chair, right arm dangling all the way to the ground, fingers connecting stiffly with the tiles; the other – the girl – was hunched forward, her chin resting on her lumpy, misshapen chest.

I altered the angle of my approach, so that I was walking directly towards them.

ACKNOWLEDGEMENTS

The British Fantasy Society published its first Yearbook in 2009; 'Unfollow' was among the stories included in it. 'Murder' was written for a collaborative project involving writers from the Manchester Writing School and practitioners from the Manchester School of Art, both part of Manchester Metropolitan University, working in association with the university library's Special Collections. A limited-edition book resulted from the collaboration, edited by artists Jonathan Carson and Rosie Miller and published by the Righton Press. 'The Obscure Bird' appeared in the British dark fiction magazine *Black Static*, edited by Andy Cox and published by TTA Press.

'Jizz' was the first of two stories written specially for this collection. In it a character, Simon, quotes some lines from *Birds by Character: The Fieldguide to Jizz Identification* (Macmillan, 1990) by Rob Hume (illustrated by Ian Wallace, Darren Rees, John Busby and Peter Partington). Thanks to Jean-Daniel Brèque for his kind assistance. 'The Bee-eater' was written for an animals-themed issue of *Succour* magazine edited by Anthony Banks.

'The Larder' was commissioned by Ellen Wiles of *Ark for A Literary Bestiary*, an 'immersive short story show' staged in Swiss Cottage Library, north-west London, in June 2015; I read the story with breaks in which Ellen Wiles performed extracts from Messiaen's *Le Merle Noir* on flute. The story, which includes quotations from *The Observer's Book of Birds' Eggs* (Frederick Warne & Co Ltd, 1954) compiled by G Evans (with illustrations by HD Swain), was later published in *The 2nd Spectral Book of Horror Stories* (Spectral Press) edited by Mark Morris.

In 'Stuffed', the second of two stories written specially for this collection, Jen and the narrator exchange three lines of dialogue from Ridley Scott's *Blade Runner* (1982). The film's screenplay is credited to Hampton Fancher and David Webb Peoples and it was adapted from the novel *Do Androids Dream of Electric Sheep* (1968) by Philip K Dick.

'Pink' was written for *Shoestring*, a magazine published by Keele University to showcase the work of its young writers. The magazine's editorial team comprised Chris Prendergast, Red Newsom, Rebecca Audra Smith and Kate Vanhinsbergh. 'Gannets' was commissioned by Manchester Literature Festival 2006 for *Original Modern Stories*, a short series of new stories by Manchester writers set in notable buildings in the city and recorded live in those buildings for broadcast on BBC Radio 4. 'The Goldfinch' was written for *British Invasion*. The idea behind this anthology – new horror stories by British writers to be published by a US press – was hatched at a convention by editors Christopher Golden, Tim Lebbon and James A Moore. It was sold to Richard Chizmar of Cemetery Dance Publications within ten minutes.

'The Kestrel and the Hawk' was written for artist, writer and lecturer Neil Coombs' journal of surrealism, *Patricide*. Solaris editor Jonathan Oliver suggested I write a story set in the Paris Métro for *The End of the Line*, an anthology of stories set on underground railway networks; 'The Lure' was the result. *Sugar Sleep* was one of three anthologies of 'slipstream' fiction edited by writer Christopher Kenworthy and published by his Barrington Books in the early 1990s; 'The Nightingale' was included in it. 'The Blue Notebooks' was written for *Manchester Central Library: A Celebration*, a live event in March 2010 to mark the library's closing for refurbishment (it reopened in 2014); the story was later published in the first issue of *Shadows & Tall Trees* edited by Michael Kelly. The story includes quotations from Agatha Christie's *The Body in the Library* (1942) and from three short stories by Jorge Luis Borges, 'The Library of Babel', 'August 25th, 1983' and 'The Other'. 'Lovebites' was written for *Bloody Vampires* edited by Charlotte Judet and published by Bobby Nayyar's Glasshouse Books, now Limehouse Books. 'The Children' was one of the new stories in *Back From the Dead: The Legacy of The Pan Book of Horror Stories* edited by Johnny Mains and published through his own Noose and Gibbet Publishing; it featured new and 'classic' stories by authors who had appeared in the original Pan series edited by Herbert Van Thal, and later Clarence Paget. Johnny Mains wrote, in his essay about Van Thal that appeared in the book, 'Clarence Paget finally got his name on the front of the book with the 26th volume and the series rapidly plummeted, both in the quality of stories (which had been poor for a while, but now only got much worse) and in sales.' My first professional publication was a story in *The 26th Pan Book of Horror Stories*.

I am grateful to all of the editors and publishers named above and to Ellen Datlow, Maxim Jakubowski and Stephen Jones, editors of anthologies in which some of these stories were reprinted.

Special thanks to Tim Shearer of Cōnfingō Publishing and to Cōnfingō art editor Zoë McLean. Thanks to my good friend Nicholas Royle and his publisher Candida Lacey at Myriad Editions, and to Myriad's creative director, Corinne Pearlman. Thanks to Matthew Frost, and to Andrew Biswell and Ian Carrington of the International Anthony Burgess Foundation. Thanks to my colleagues at the Manchester Writing School and in the English Department of Manchester Metropolitan University, in particular, on this occasion, Livi Michael, James Draper, Joe Stretch and Adam O'Riordan. Thanks to my agent, John Saddler, and to David Rose, Conrad Williams, Claire Dean and John Oakey.

Special thanks also to Ros, and to my mum, my sisters Julie and Joanna, to Simon, and to Kate, and to my children, Charlie and Bella.

'Unfollow', copyright © Nicholas Royle 2009, was first published in *British Fantasy Society Yearbook 2009* (British Fantasy Society)

'Murder', copyright © Nicholas Royle 2009, was first published in *Stilled Lives* (Righton Press) edited by Carson & Miller

'The Obscure Bird', copyright © Nicholas Royle 2010, was first published in *Black Static* 18

'Jizz', copyright © Nicholas Royle 2017, original to this collection

'The Bee-eater', copyright © Nicholas Royle 2008, was first published in *Succour* Spring/Summer 2008

'The Larder', copyright © Nicholas Royle 2015, was first published in *The 2nd Spectral Book of Horror Stories* (Spectral Press) edited by Mark Morris

'Stuffed', copyright © Nicholas Royle 2017, original to this collection

'Pink', copyright © Nicholas Royle 2010, was first published in *Shoestring* May 2010

'Gannets', copyright © Nicholas Royle 2006, was first broadcast on BBC Radio 4

'The Goldfinch', copyright © Nicholas Royle 2008, was first published in *British Invasion* (Cemetery Dance Publications) edited by Christopher Golden, Tim Lebbon & James A Moore

'The Kestrel and the Hawk', copyright © Nicholas Royle 2010, was first published in *Patricide 02: Seaside Surrealism* (Dark Windows Press) edited by Neil Coombs

'The Lure', copyright © Nicholas Royle 2010, was first published in *The End of the Line* (Solaris) edited by Jonathan Oliver

'The Nightingale', copyright © Nicholas Royle 1993, was first published in *Sugar Sleep* (Barrington Books) edited by Chris Kenworthy

'The Blue Notebooks', copyright © Nicholas Royle 2010, was first published in *Shadows & Tall Trees* 1

'Lovebites', copyright © Nicholas Royle 2010, was first published in *Bloody Vampires* (Glasshouse Books) edited by Charlotte Judet

'The Children', copyright © Nicholas Royle 2010, was first published in *Back From the Dead: The Legacy of The Pan Book of Horror Stories* (Noose and Gibbet Publishing) edited by Johnny Mains